Feeder
Chronicles of the Soul Eaters
Lucinda Moebius

Feeder
Copyright ©2014 by Lucinda Moebius

Haven Novels 2011
Haven Novels
www.lucindamoebius.com
First Hardcover Edition: 2014
First Paperback Edition: 2014
First E-Book Edition: 2014

Feeder

a novel by Lucinda Moebius. -1st. ed. p.cm.
ISBN-13: 9780615968322
Printed in the United States of America
Haven Novels

Chapter One

SAL WAS NEARLY BURIED in old rags, sheets of newspaper and cardboard. I could barely see her blue eyes shining through the garbage covering her body. Burying yourself in garbage is a good way to keep warm. Sometimes. More often than not you end up frostbitten and nearly dead. Much like Sal was now. I crouched down and brushed the debris from her face. Her breath steamed as she released it. I could almost taste the sourness of her energy as it oozed out of her pores.

Bringing my face close to hers, I breathed in her life-force. Despite the sourness, her energy tasted good. I brought my lips down on hers and breathed in her life. For a moment she struggled against me, but I could feel the release when she finally accepted the death I was bringing her. I hadn't really fed for days and it took everything I had to not suck her dry. Sal deserved a little dignity in her death. She was still breathing, barely, when I pulled away. Her breath was coming in short, shallow gasps and her skin was a grayish-yellow shade.

I pulled my cell phone out of my pocket, the one they gave me at the shelter when they told me the streets weren't safe and dialed the only number to which the battered device would connect.

"9-1-1," the woman sounded tired. "Do you need Police, Fire or Medical?"

"Medical." I'm old hat at this. I think the 911 operators can even recognize my voice. Maybe I'm exaggerating a little bit. It's not like I had reason to call every day but living on the streets did allow me to witness more crime than the average person. I'm young and healthy and have owned the streets since I was fourteen. Since I don't sleep I spend most of my time wandering the streets and looking for prey. The streets offered everything I needed to survive.

"Sal's not breathin' too good." I explained. It always helps if I don't come off sounding too intelligent. No one expects a street girl to have an IQ above 180.

It took nearly ten minutes for the fire department to find us. The paramedics recognized me, not surprising since Feeders always recognize each other. Sick and dying people always bleed energy and the medical field draws in Feeders like rotting flesh draws flies. Despite the IV and warming blankets the two men provided her, I seriously doubted Sal would make it to the hospital alive. At least she would die warm and pain free.

Once the ambulance and police cars left I was alone in the dark alley. Sal was an old, self-medicating schizophrenic and her energy was fractured and slightly toxic. I was already feeling the effects of trying to digest the energy as my body forced the toxins out of my pores. I rearranged the rags and cardboard to offer extra support for my head and curled up in the nest. The seizure would only last a few moments and I didn't want to wake up with injuries. I wasn't out for long, but I was drowsy and achy when the seizure was over. My stomach rolled as I turned over and tried to sit up. The shelter food I had eaten earlier in the day made its reappearance as I heaved into the pile of rags. The mess didn't do anything to improve the smell of sweat and bodily fluids already inherent in a street dwellers nest. I had to get away before the smell made everything worse.

I used the brick wall as a support and forced my way to my feet. No one was around when I staggered from the alley. Lights and sirens scattered street dwellers like rats running from a flood. It wouldn't take long for the curious to come to investigate Sal's nest. Her habits were well known and some hopeful addict would be combing through the trash looking for rocks. I had enough energy now I could go find healthier prey. Addict energy works when I'm starving, but the side-effects from their toxic bleeding always makes me feel hung-over so I try not to feed on them too often.

I walked to the TriMet stop, three blocks away. Pulling my pass from under my clothes, I made sure it was visible as it dangled from the chain and rested against the front of my shirt. Sal's energy burned through me, giving me strength and clarity. My stomach was finally settling and I was starting to get hungry.

The city was just starting to come alive as early morning commuters made their way to the train station. It was still too early for the business professionals, secretaries, office workers and such so I joined the crush of service workers heading to coffee shops, bakeries and restaurants in the heart of the city. Every one of them gave me a wide berth, not because I was dirty or smelled bad, but because from their perspective it looked like I was blind and I have learned most humans fear anything they perceived as different. It's true my eyes are milky white, but I can see. I see in ways no human can ever imagine.

The humans were bleeding energy. It wept out of them like a colored mist. There was a group of utility worker huddled together around one of the center poles, trying not to bump elbows with the other occupants of the crowded car. I edged closer to them, tasting the bitter-sweet tang of their energy. If I'm close enough to the humans I can draw their energy into my body like humans absorb light and oxygen. Physical contact allows me to draw the energy directly from my prey. Given enough time I can suck a human dry, not even leaving enough energy for the prey to keep his heart beating. It doesn't take much energy to keep me going, though. I feed on the residual energy being cast off by humans as they go through their day. It's enough to keep me going between feedings. But sometimes I need more. There are many creatures out there like me. Monsters who draw their energy from humans, but many of them don't completely drain their prey as often as I do. Some of them team up to give themselves enough power to overwhelm their victims and even then, they aren't usually powerful enough to do more than weaken their prey. I only know of a handful of my kind capable of completely draining our prey.

I rarely draw the energy directly from the body of humans I knew, but Sal was dying anyway and I was just so hungry I couldn't help myself. Feeding leaves marks, usually only noticeable by other feeders. There's always plenty of prey so I don't need to worry about competition from others like me, but humans tend to notice a pattern of unexplained deaths and, unless there's a natural explanation for the occurrence, they tend to start looking for an explanation outside of nature. Feeders rarely liked to draw attention to themselves and humans looking for explanations beyond nature brings too much attention to us.

My apartment was only a few blocks off the main TriMet line and by the time the train pulled up to my stop I was feeling strong enough to walk home. I suppose I could have taken the bus, but I was feeling so full of energy I needed to work some of it off. It was going to take a little while to process the energy I siphoned off my prey.

Carefully opening my door, I slipped inside the small, one-bedroom basement apartment. The upstairs neighbors were late sleepers and frequently complained of my early morning habits. I try to be quiet when I come in, but sometimes I'm so sick from the night's feeding it takes all my effort to get the door unlocked and closed behind me before collapsing. Worrying about whether I am waking the neighbors with slamming doors and seizures is the least of my concerns.

The seizures weren't very frequent and I wasn't overly concerned since I usually had enough warning they were coming to find a safe place before I lost it. I wouldn't have them at all if I was more selective in my diet. They were a result of my body trying to sort the useful energy from toxic elements attached to the ions I bleed from my prey. At least I think that was the cause, there aren't very many entries about my kind in the medical books. Not many at all.

I'm an efficient Feeder. I can draw energy from any area of the human body. I don't need to tap into the brain and central nervous system to draw core energy like so many others of my species. My prey rarely knows when I've feasted on them and they continue with their lives not realizing they've given me a tiny portion of their soul, unless I consumed them completely.

My body was craving food. Real food, not energy. I needed to eat something to replace the calories I lost because of the seizure. The human part of me needed sustenance to survive. There was a shelter about seven blocks from my apartment. The food wasn't that great, but I could barely taste it anyway and I learned to eat it fast enough to ignore the texture. I thought about heading to the shelter to get some breakfast, but I had already made enough noise coming into the apartment so I decided not to push it.

There's a kitchen in my apartment. Well, there's a stove and a fridge in one corner of the studio, but I don't keep very much food there. I opened the fridge and pulled out a plastic container full of bean soup from behind the half gallon of milk. I dumped about half of it into a saucepan and plopped it onto the stove. It only took a few minutes for bubbles to appear in the thick sauce. Giving the soup a quick stir to distribute the heat, I carried the pan to the little glass-top table and sat at the only chair. I sliced a hunk off the round loaf of bread sitting at the center of the table and used it to push beans onto my spoon. At least the food the Sisters brought me was more palatable than the shelter food.

I took special care with cleaning and putting away my dishes because I knew Sister Agnes and Sister Sofia were planning on visiting this afternoon and they didn't need to see my mess. After my shower I stripped my bed, bundled my dirty laundry in a canvas bag and placed it beside the door. I remade the bed and made sure everything was spotless. It was important to foster the illusion I was just a little blind girl determined to make it on her own. The apartment was just another illusion I created to hide my true being.

Sister Agnes would know I was expecting her. She knew my secrets, at least some of them anyway, because Agnes and I shared the same secrets. She was centuries old and I was barely twenty, but we came from the same family. Her appetite was insatiable, but she had a ready supply of prey at the asylum.

It was difficult being Agnes' special pet, but at least if she was watching over me my grandfather wouldn't be able to find me and use me for his own purposes. Agnes promised she would protect me from my grandfather. She had been hiding me all my life and I had learned to trust her, at least with this area of my life. I wasn't ready to face my grandfather, yet. He had plans for me. Plans I wanted no part of.

Chapter Two

I SLEPT FOR ABOUT an hour, if you can call what I do sleep. The best I could do was lay down and allow my body to relax. I focused on the energy I consumed, trying to distribute it throughout my body. My heart beat slowed and my breathing evened out as the energy settled into my chest and spread to my limbs. I could feel strength filling my core and spreading to the rest of my body.

My bed was a simple padded mat supported by slats in a wooden frame. The parish gave it to me when I refused the offer of a full sized, pillow-top mattress. I didn't require a comfortable resting place. I just needed a safe place for my body to process the energy I consumed from my prey.

I couldn't stay in the bed very long. Soon I was up and pacing the short length of the apartment. It was early enough in the day I thought about heading to the park to see if I could spend some time feeding, but I didn't want to risk not making it back to the apartment before one o'clock. I knew the sisters were planning to arrive just after they finished serving lunch at the shelter and Agnes was notorious for letting herself into my apartment and waiting until I arrived home. Agnes didn't need a key to get into my apartment and no matter how long I stayed out I knew she would be there, in my apartment, waiting for me.

I decided the best way to fill the time waiting for her was with words. The last time she had visited Agnes had brought me a 1600s treatise called *The Were*. The narrow, leather-bound volume was printed on velum and the pages crackled under my fingers. The script glowed as each word hovered off the page. I don't see so much in color spectrum as I do in layers. Light bended around the energy of the page and I sensed the words. I used my fingers to feel around the edges of the marks on the velum to clarify meaning. It was more difficult to read the spidery script and awkward spelling of the words, but the subject matter was informative enough to keep my interest. Plus, the author had illustrated each point in the book with colorful, and sometimes terrifying, images.

There so much humans don't understand about our species and, like any creature trying to learn about a subject, there are many instances where superstition and fear filled in the blanks. The priest who had written this treatise must have had a greater understanding of our species. His treatment of the mythology from many cultures and comparative analysis of feeder behavior gave credence to his research. Of all the books I have read on Vampyres, his explanation came closest to what we really are. The only problem I had with his writing was he ended each description with the various ways to kill a creature like me. I'm not keen on the idea of giving humans the knowledge to kill me. Most vampyres try to create the illusion we can't be killed.

Maybe vampyre isn't the best way to describe what I am. I prefer to think of myself as a Were. Were-creatures have been ingrained into human mythology since story telling was first established to teach and communicate ideas. Perhaps our ancestors weren't as careful with their abilities in the earliest phases of the evolutionary process, or maybe in the early years the Were and the humans had a more symbiotic relationship. Whatever the reason, humans know we exist. The stories about us have grown and spread like some fantastic, fanciful game of telephone.

This priest, writing at the tail end of the dark ages, came close to a description of who we are. He described the various shapes we can shift into and our ability to consume our victims. Unfortunately, he seemed to focus on the most horrific aspects of our species. I mean, every culture has their psychopaths. Ted Bundy was a human, so was Al Capone. Vlad the Impaler was one of us, but I think that's common knowledge. Most humans don't realize the true nature of this creature, though. They either dismiss the stories about his blood-sucking nature to myth or believe he was just a mortal who enjoyed torturing his victims and watching them die.

It's difficult to sort the truth from the legend because some of my people did drink blood and eat the flesh of their prey, but we aren't the only monsters out there with this perversion. We aren't any more prone to aberrant behavior then humans with psychotic, serial killing, behaviors. It's not necessary to consume the flesh and blood of the creature to absorb the energy, but the victim always seems to cling to the last vestiges of their soul in the moments of death so it's easier to feed on energy when you draw away their life-sustaining elements. We weren't born with sharp teeth and claws, but according to the pictures in the book some of my forefathers created weapons designed to puncture veins and arteries of the prey so they could feast on all elements of the flesh.

The priest listed all the names my kind were called by according to his understanding. Vampyre, werewolf, demon, monster, witch, soul-eater, devil, the list went on for pages. He didn't distinguish between the differences between the kinds of creatures. Even I knew there is a difference between witches and vampyres. In his mind all energy creatures were evil and needed to be destroyed.

I was in the middle of an especially gruesome description of the judgment and execution of a suspected witch when the sound of a car door closing drew me away from my reading. The book was hidden away in the bottom drawer of my wooden dresser and I was at the door before the Sisters were even halfway up the walk. Despite the advanced age of her current physical body, Agnes was surprisingly spry and proceeded the much younger Sophia down the stairs to the door of my apartment. The cancer in Sophia's hip was spreading much faster than the young woman realized. I could almost taste the rotting of her energy through the wood frame of the door. Even with treatment, I doubted she had much more than six months to live. Less, if Agnes kept feeding on her at the rate she was going.

Sophia's burden wasn't lighter despite her illness. She carried a box of food and supplies into the room and placed it on the table. I watched her as she silently limped around the room, putting items away, gathering stray articles of clothing and dusting surfaces. I always made sure to leave streaks and strays around to maintain the illusion of blindness.

Sister Sophia was under a vow of silence, one of the many steps to taking her final vows. I didn't want to speak to her because she didn't think I could see her nods and gestures she used to communicate and there wasn't really anything I wanted to talk to Agnes about within earshot of the novice, so we sat in silence while Sophia made her way around the room.

There wasn't much work to do and it wasn't long before Sophia gathered the bag containing my dirty laundry and carried it up the stairs. I waited until I heard her heavy tread on the top step before I turned my attention to Agnes.

"Why don't you just heal her, already?" My voice was probably a little challenging. I really didn't like the way Agnes seemed to revel in Sophia's pain.

Agnes' tongue darted out of her mouth like a snake testing the air. I wondered if the woman could taste energy the same way I saw it. She smiled as she plucked the thoughts out of my mind.

"I want the miracle to be well documented." Agnes reached across the table and grasped my hand. I could feel the ball of energy close to her heart. The blue light swirled around her chest and pulsated with each drum of her heartbeat. "Her body will be a perfect vessel for my power and her healing will be the first miracle associated with my death. These little mortals are so quaint in their customs. I like the idea of this vessel being immortalized in their books."

The dry skin of her hands chaffed against mine and my own energy throbbed in my chest and head. I drew my hand away from hers and pushed my fingers against my throbbing temples. Pulling my energy into my core, I drew a shield between myself and the woman standing in front of me. I could feel her assaulting the edges of my shield, pushing her energy against me. Her energy crept around me with probing fingers, tickling and pressing into my shield. At first, I let her seek with no resistance, then I started pushing back. She pushed harder, but I thrust against her encroaching energy. Her upper lip glistened with sweat and her eyes hardened. I knew the moment she realized I wasn't letting her in by the great exhalation of air bursting from her chest, causing her to lose her concentration. She smiled and patted my arm.

"Good job, Maria Christine." She sat on the edge of the bed, the only place to sit in my apartment other than the chair at the table. "You're becoming much better at shielding your energy. You need to keep your shield in place as much as possible. Hunters won't be able to distinguish your energy from humans as long as you keep it hidden."

My thoughts immediately went to the leather-bound book hidden in my drawer. The image of a woman writhing in pain as flames danced around her body flashed through my mind. Definitely not the most pleasant way to die. My mortal body was just as prone to injury as any human. This fragile flesh could be pierced by bullets or stabbed with sword and knife. The bullets didn't need to be silver and the sword didn't need to be imbued with some mystical power to tear through my flesh, they just had to hit a vital organ to kill me, otherwise I could use my energy to seal the wound and repair the injury. The thought of someone hell-bent on hunting me down and striving to separate my head from my spinal cord with a sword just because I was born a Were was enough to motivate me to learn to hide my energy behind a shield.

I could hear the shuffling steps of Sister Sophia on the stairs. Moving away from Agnes, I opened the little cupboard above the sink and ran my fingers over the canned goods Sophia had placed there. Agnes described each can as my fingers traced the lettering on the labels. I would bring most of the cans to the shelter to be dropped in the donation bin once the two women left. They always brought more food then I could eat in a week, but I had to maintain the illusion of humanity for Sophia's sake. At least they didn't bring me meat products. I couldn't bring myself to consume the flesh of animals. Every time I thought of the blood flowing through the flesh my stomach roiled. I hated meat.

Sophia was pale and glistening by the time she made it back to the room. I would have offered her a seat, but I knew she believed her suffering was just another test of her conviction to her faith and the ensuing back and forth, albeit a silent one, would be frustrating and uncomfortable. Agnes directed Sophia to the door and giving me a brief farewell pregnant with the promise of a return for more instruction. She turned and followed the woman out of the room.

The apartment felt charged after she was gone and every hair on my body seemed to stand on end. I tried returning to my studies, but I couldn't focus on my reading so I tucked the book back in its place in my drawer and changed into my hunting clothes.

It was late in the day and the temperature had started to drop. The cold didn't affect me as much as it did humans, but it would look odd if I was wandering the streets in sparse clothing. I pulled my black sweatshirt over the black, long-sleeved, turtle-neck. My black pants and shoes completed my outfit. No amount of black clothing could hide my pale, white skin, but the hood of the sweatshirt pulled over my close-cropped, sandy brown hair would hide me nearly completely from anyone but the most astute searchers. I didn't hunt in the dark because of any fear of being destroyed by sunlight. I hunted in the dark because it was easier to remain hidden and spring on my prey unaware.

Chapter Three

CROUCHING BEHIND THE BLUE metal dumpster, I waited for the group of college kids to stagger by the opening of the alley. One of the boys hollered at his friends to wait a minute and turned into the alley where I was hiding. I heard the distinct sound of a zipper being lowered and the hiss and splash as he relieved himself against the brick wall. His friends didn't wait for him and it wasn't long before we were alone in the alley. I could almost taste the sour scent of his energy as he realized his friends might actually leave him behind. He wasn't even comforted by the knowledge he had the keys to the car in the front pocket of his pants. I was able to easily pick the information from his alcohol-soaked brain.

I stepped from behind the dumpster just as he finished zipping the front of his jeans. I knew from the first moment I felt him I was going to drain him dry and I really didn't want to deal with his exposed flesh as he collapsed to the ground. The man was turning towards the opening of the alley so I kicked a pebble against the metal frame of the dumpster. The noise caused him to start and turn towards me. I made a point of appearing to stagger in imitation of his own intoxicated state. His eyes widened in realization as I stepped into the square of light cast from a window of the apartment facing the alley. I allowed him a moment to drink in the image I was projecting for him and stepped back into the shadows.

My real form wasn't all that pretty. My cheekbones were cast at a high angle and my milky eyes were too wide-set. I was also quite bony and angular with hard, wiry muscles. But, it's not too hard for me to project any shape I want and a beautiful, buxom blonde nearly falling out of a low cut, short dress is usually enough to catch any man's eye. I knew he was drunk enough not to think about why a woman would be wandering around half-dressed in the middle of January. My impression was confirmed when he stepped into the shadows to follow me.

"Hey, pretty lady," his whistling whisper carried to my ear. "Why are you trying to hide?"

My tongue darted out, catching his flavor in the air. I waited until he was right beside the dumpster before I made my strike. He didn't even stand a chance. For a moment he struggled against the strength of my arms, but I had him pinned to the ground and was sitting on his chest before he could gasp for breath. I grabbed his head between my hands and placed my lips against his. It was a sweet, lasting kiss as I drew his energy from the core of his heart. I drew out the last spark of life from his body and separated the toxic portions of his soul from the fire of his blue energy. He was young and his energy was strong and tasted sweet, but the sourness was still there. I could feel the pain he caused those girls; the young coed, the chubby, drunk girl at the bar, his high school girlfriend. They had said no, but he had broken them. And there were others. I took their pain and combined it with the flavor of the alcohol in his blood. Exhaling all the pain the girls felt, all the hopelessness, guilt and despair, I purged it all back into his fragile human flesh. The beat of his heart faltered and stuttered as I drained the last of his energy from his body. Tracing my tongue around his lips one last time, I tasted his sweetness and savored his last breath.

Noise from the street drew me up short. His friends were coming back for him. I could hear their drunken laughter and stumbling footsteps as they called his name. Disengaging, I sprang to my feet and leapt for the second story balcony. The wrought iron barely made any noise as I crawled over the edge and made my way to the ladder leading to the third floor. Within seconds I was up the ladder and onto the access leading to the roof. I could have moved faster, but I didn't want to make any noise and I haven't quite learned how to focus my energy to bend the air around me and levitate off the ground while keeping my body stable. I had seen Agnes do it a few times, but it took focus to master the technique and I didn't have that kind of focus.

I had chosen this alley and this building because the brick façade extended beyond the roofline. The elaborate cornices supported sweeping gargoyles with arching wings curling behind their twisted backs. My body quivered with suppressed energy as I leaned against the stone arch of the gargoyles back. I had time. It would be a while before his friends found his body and even longer before one of them would think to call the police. His life-force was completely mine now. No amount of CPR would bring him back.

It felt so good, his energy coursing through my body. I hadn't feasted like that in months. I wanted to stay and savor the feeling, but I was too close to his body. There were more than just feeders out there in the dark. I pulled the energy into my core and pushed away from the cold stone of the gargoyle. The sound of an ambulance sirens covered my footsteps across the rooftop. After a few steps I had built up enough momentum to leap across the divide from one roof to another. I could feel the power building around me as I crossed the rooftops. The energy was so strong it was a fire in my chest. I could only go so far on the rooftops and I had to zigzag to find buildings close to the same height so I wouldn't have to adjust my equilibrium with each leap.

The ambient temperature dropped at least five degrees as I got closer to the river. I thought about dropping down by the Burnside bridge and finding another energy source, but I was so full from the boy any more feeding tonight would just be gluttonous. Between the full moon and the city lights, the river glowed with a silver incandescent light. I made my way along the shore to the shipping yard. Barges lined the docks piled high with shipping containers. I stayed to the shadows, avoiding the feebly peering flashlights of the guards.

It was easy to slip down the dock and on to a container ship without the guards noticing me. I was fast and quiet and most guards are too lazy to explore the ships much beyond the furthest edge of their flashlight beam. Leaping from one barge to the next, I made my way to the last ship in the yard. I found a short stack of containers in the middle of the barge and, rolling up my sweatshirt as a cushion for my head, stretched out on top of the cold, metal surface.

I relaxed my body into the power of the energy I had just consumed. The sound of the river was soothing and rich, pushing the weight of the city off my shoulders. I was far enough away from the city lights to actually see some stars. The legends tell of Were losing control of their human form and hunting indiscriminately through the night. I never felt the effect of the moon and I have never lost control on a h. Simply put, the reason I hunt more often during the full moon is it's easier to see when the moon brightens the landscape. More humans are out and about during the full moon. Stupid humans doing stupid things make easy hunting. Thieves climbing on rooftops are my favorite. It's easy to make it look like they slipped off the roof and broke something vital.

I licked my lips, remembering the taste of the man and the strength of his energy flowing through me. His death would be ruled a sudden heart attack. Such a shame for a healthy-looking young man. It's not hard to stop the electrical impulse from the brain to the heart when you have such an intimate connection to the body. I didn't need skin-to-skin contact to drain a person of their energy, but it was easier to control the manner of death if I actually touched their skin. It also gave me more control over timing of the feeding. I didn't like to drain them too quickly. Drinking energy too fast gave me headaches and could sometimes bring on my seizures. Besides, the type of prey I hunted usually deserved long, lingering deaths.

I hate creeps who like to watch people suffer for their own pleasure. Giving cruel people back a little of what they give victims is one of my few joys in life. I like to think my feeding habits make the world a little more pleasant then when I started. The first time I completely drained another person of their soul was when I was eight years old.

I was a foster child since birth. No one knew the origin of my birth, well no one but me. There were a few who suspected and a few more who made educated guesses, but I was the only living person who knew exactly where I came from. My mother is a descendant of one of the strongest Soul Eaters ever born. Her father, my grandfather, kept her sheltered, knowing she had the potential for great power. But, when you keep a jewel locked in a tower, away from temptation, it stokes the desire of every thief and vagabond and fires the imagination. My mother was seduced during her first heat by one of her guards. He fled the scene of the crime before it was discovered, though. My mother, fifteen and pregnant, was left alone in her father's home. She told him nothing of her pregnancy and continued to feast on the souls of the victims he brought her. She never learned to control the energy of her prey and savor the feeding. As a result, I was not protected from the energy being drawn into her body. I absorbed the energy and knowledge of all those souls. They infested my form and imbued me with power even beyond my understanding.

For my mother's sixteenth birthday my father captured a witch. He showed my mother how to feed on the soul of another Were, drawing in the power and knowledge of her prey into herself. My grandfather should have been more observant of both his daughter and the witch. The power of the witch fractured as my mother feasted. My mother had successfully hid her pregnancy for nearly eight months and I was almost fully formed. By this point I was aware enough of my own abilities to draw most of the witch's knowledge and power into my tiny body. I become even more powerful than the combination of my genetic ancestors. All the knowledge of my forbearers exploded through me and I suddenly knew. I more than knew. I was awake and I was alive and I was ready.

It was too much for my mother. She became wild and crazy. Lunging at the witch, my mother used her teeth to rip out the woman's throat. I was aware of every moment, every thought, every fracture in my mother's mind. The warmth of the witch's blood flowing down my mother's throat became a warmth in my tiny, barely-formed throat. I could taste the metallic tang of the iron in the woman's blood and it made me sick. I had to escape. The guards came and dragged my mother to the dungeon. I know it's strange to think of buildings having dungeons in these modern days, but my grandfather is a wealthy and powerful man and he has a way of getting what he wants. His house is hidden in the deepest recess of a wooded copse. The number of secrets buried with the bodies in those woods defy imagination.

The moon dipped below my sight-line and darkness rolled across the river. As the night sounds echoed across the water I drank in the energy of the night. It was quiet and the waves lapping against the barge gently rocked me, allowing me to focus on the energy coursing through my body. I closed my eyes and allowed the night to take me.

Chapter Four

THE SOUNDS OF THE regions wildlife accompanying the rising sun drew me from my reflection. As the sun broached the horizon the calls of birds waiting for the casting from the boats signaled the hurried birth of the day. I had lingered too long and I knew I would never be able to sneak off the dock without drawing attention to myself. A scurrying and scuffing noise gave me an idea, though.

Gathering my energy, I focused on the tiny form just at the edges of my sight. My mind formed the image and forced my body into the dimensions of the creature. Becoming a Were is more illusion than anything else anyway. My overall body mass can't change. My stunted, four-legged form was surrounded by an energy force roughly the size and shape of my original dimensions. Other Were would be able to discern my true form and since many humans have some elements of Were sense it's not unusual to hear them talk about strange animal, human hybrids and witnessing attacks by half human, half animal creatures.

I skittered down the side of the crates and leaped from the barge onto the dock. The morning dock crew was just coming on shift and I must have startled one of the workers. I dodged a heavy boot as the sound of a harsh curse assaulted my ears. A gap between two boards allowed me to escape the congestion of the dock and I scurried along the support beams beneath the main frame. A few inches from the end of the dock I decided I would be safer in a different form since most humans don't like rodents. I changed my form to resemble a cat. A feline is faster anyway and I figured I could get far enough into the tree-line on the shore before anyone could capture me.

I was away from the docks and in the safety of the trees before anyone could react to my sudden appearance. Once I was amongst the trees and safely hidden from prying eyes I reverted back to my own shape. I could have stayed in Were-shape until I made it home, but it's easier to stay undetected in human form.

As I climbed the gentle slope leading from the edge of the river to a slight hill I realized I was very near the chapel where I was found as an infant. Crossing the park at an angle, I made my way to the tiny rectory. The squat, stone building nestled beside a large cathedral. Angled slightly behind the rectory was an ancient graveyard dominated by large, heavy headstones intermingling with winged cherubs and saintly statues. Early morning mist obscured the footings of the stones and sunlight dancing on beads of dew brightened the landscape.

I wandered amongst the tombs until I found the sweeping memorial to an ancient family. The name Williams figured prominently in this section of the graveyard. I knew I wasn't related to any of the family buried there, even though I shared their last name. Maria Christina Williams. I was named by the Parish Priest who found me at the foot of this very grave. Maria for the Holy Mother, Christina for the faith he believed saved me and Williams because he assumed the person who left me here had some connection to the family. None of it is true. I was saved by an old crone.

I was born in the depths of the dungeon, falling from my mother's womb to the arms of a woman who had been called in to assuage her mad ravings. My grandfather was far away at the time, dealing with the consequences of the madness of my mother. The midwife barely survived touching me when her hands cradled my slick, quivering body. Only her own power as a feeder prevented me from consuming her completely. She realized what I was from the moment I was born. Wrapping me tightly in bundles and tucking me into the bosom of her dress, the nursemaid smuggled me out of the dungeon, leaving my bleeding, half-crazed mother imprisoned in the dank cell under her father's home.

I traced the letters on the cold stone marble of the memorial. I remembered how cold the ground was when the old lady had placed me at the foot of the headstone. She stayed beside me, allowing me to feed on her energy to keep me warm and safe until I could be found. I remember the warmth of her body as she held me and soothed my trembling body with whispered songs. Her energy sustained me until I was found and when she gave me the last bit of her life-force her body faded into dust. I still carry a piece of her with me. Every once in a while, I hear her voice calling to me, warning, guiding, quietly whispering in my ear. She is wise and had lived many lifetimes. Her spirit strengthens my soul every day.

I dropped my hand away from the stone and turned back towards the trees. A shadow stepped out of the edge of the woods and walked towards the graveyard. The form was quickly followed by two others. The animals looked odd together. A fox and a cougar walking side by side and a raven flying over their head. I could see the shadow of their human form deep within their energy. As they emerged from the edge of the trees they melted out of Were-shape and became human. There was only one reason they would be here now. It wasn't unusual for Were to band together, it made hunting for prey easier, but Were species didn't mix. It took strong coven bonds for Were of different abilities to band together and there was only one coven strong enough to overcome species bias. As far as I knew I was the only Were in history capable of taking multiple forms and I always walked alone.

I stood frozen to the spot in front of the grave, unable to move. It wasn't fear. I don't think I even know what fear feels like. I think I was just curious. As the threesome approached I shifted my weight forward on the balls of my feet and shook my arms to relax the muscles. I can move fast and I'm strong. Taking on three Were might be stretching even my abilities, though. I wanted to know why a cat, fox and bird were banding together, so I didn't run.

The cat took the lead as they approached. They stopped few feet from me, each of them eying me warily. Leaning against the memorial, I attempted to take on a casual stance, letting them know I wasn't really worried about them.

"Maria Christina," the cougar's voice was strangely soft, almost as if he was trying to sneak up on me. "I'm here to take you home."

I didn't say anything in response. There wasn't really anything to say to this kind of statement. I never really had a home. Even the apartment I was in now wasn't really a home so much as a place to keep the books Agnes brought me.

They just stood there staring at me. What were they expecting? Did they want me to grovel at their feet and thank them for offering me a home? I snorted and pushed myself away from the stone at my back. I thought about just turning and walking away, but I had a feeling they had more to say and if I walked away they might actually follow me.

The cougar kept his gaze steady but the other two were exchanging glances. I had a feeling things weren't going the way they expected.

"Listen, child," he was obviously trying again. I wondered exactly how old he was to call me child. His human form looked fit and young, broad shouldered, dark, tall. All the things humans found attractive. The only indication of his age was a touch of silver in his black hair at his temples. "I'm not going to hurt you. Your grandfather sent me to bring you home. He's been searching for you for a long time. Don't worry, I won't let anything bad happen to you."

If I had been frightened his voice would have done nothing to reassure me. I smiled and shook my head.

"I'm not interested." My answer seemed to disarm the two Were behind him. They exchanged nervous glances and then moved to spread out behind the cougar. I shifted my stance, drawing myself up to my full height. I must admit it probably wasn't that impressive since I am barely above five feet, but I wanted to let them know I was aware of what they were doing. Both of them stopped and studied me, their eyes flickering back and forth as if they were trying to decide what to do.

"I'm not going anywhere." I said it quietly, without any emotional infliction.

The cougar smiled. I could see his tongue pressing against the white of his teeth. "Maria, you belong with your family." He took a step towards me and reached out as if to touch my arm. I stood my ground. "You have a brother and a sister who want their older sister home with them. Your grandfather will provide everything you ever want or need. Your home is with us. We're waiting for you."

"And what about my mother?"

The cougar shuddered, but then seemed to remember himself. The smile was back. "She's getting stronger every day. I'm sure she wants you back home, just like the rest of us."

"I've lived the past nineteen years without my grandfather." I didn't break eye-contact with the cougar. "I'm pretty sure I can get along fine without him."

"He loves you, Maria." The smile was gone. "If he would have known your mother was pregnant he would've never let her feed on that witch. You would've been born at the house and raised in comfort and security your entire life. He can't fix what happened in your past, but he can give you anything you need now."

"You don't get it," my voice was a low growl. "I don't need anything from him."

This time there was no subtle shifting to the side. The raven and fox blurred into motion, each attacking from the side. Between one blink and the next I leapt from the ground to the top of the memorial and then to the roof of a mausoleum nearly fifty yards away. A comedy of errors played out on the grounds as the fox and raven collided and swiped briefly at each other's faces. It was obvious any truce they had was tenuous at best. With a growl, the cougar forced them apart and they spread out to search for me.

My perch on the top of the mausoleum afforded me some protection. I was far enough away to watch the search progress, but I knew if I stayed put they would find me eventually. There weren't really many places to hide on the flat rooftop and the early morning sun was burning off the last of the mist floating up from the river. It was becoming apparent I would either need to confront the Were searching for me or I would have to run away and hide. Running away would only mean they would follow and I would eventually need to confront them. Confronting them now, when I didn't know enough about them to weigh their strengths, could mean I could lose and I hate the idea of losing.

Chapter Five

THE THREE OF THEM were spread far apart, searching amongst the graves. The raven was near the mausoleum, but his eyes were searching the ground. It looked like he was spending more time glancing up to see what the others were doing then actually searching for me. His eyes were on the cougar when he crossed under my hiding place. With slow, deliberate motions I pulled myself into a position to drop down on top of him. A sudden piercing shriek rang through the graveyard and halted my movements.

In my focus on the raven I had lost track of the other Were. Both the raven and I turned our attention to where the shriek came from. Someone had joined us in the graveyard. I looked up just in time to see the cat's head separate from his shoulders and fly five feet through the air, landing at the foot of a grave. Whatever killed the creature was invisible to my eye. The body of the cat lay crumpled on the ground at the base of a small monument. His energy force became a green mist, hovering over his body for a brief moment. I knew I could reach out and draw the energy from the body, but there was something out there capable of killing Were and I didn't want to draw attention to myself. I stared, mesmerized by the ball of green light hovering over the body. My tongue darted out of my mouth, trying to taste the essence of the soul. It seemed such a loss to allow all that energy to just disperse into the energy of the universe.

The green mass wasn't acting right. I kept expecting it to expand and disperse, but instead it condensed into nearly a spherical shape and seemed to chase after the fleeing forms of the raven and the fox. The light caught up to them as they entered the edge of the wood, but it halted suddenly and disappeared. It was so quick I almost missed the dark shadow form outlined by the light. The energy ball had entered something. It wasn't absorbed slowly, like it would have been if a feeder took it. The ball disappeared as if it entered a door and didn't come out again.

I didn't know what type of creature was chasing down the Were, but I knew I didn't need to be around when it came back. Turning, I moved to the other side of the mausoleum, wanting to at least put the building between me and the creature. I was just about ready to lower myself over the edge of the building when movement beneath me stayed my action. A man, dressed in the black robes of a priest initiate, stood directly beneath me. His blue eyes stared up at me, wide with surprise and wonder.

"Get down here."

His voice was gentle and yet the command was so compelling there was nothing I could do but comply. I dropped from the mausoleum, a height of a little over thirty feet, and landed on the balls of my feet. The Priest seemed unsurprised by my actions and motioned for me to follow him. Again, I had the compulsion to obey and I fell into step behind him as he led me to the grave where the cat had fallen.

I was expecting to see the decapitated body curled on the ground, but nothing was there. The grass where the body had been lying had a slight grey cast to it. Swirls of grey dust danced around my shoes as we stepped over the spot where the head had fallen. He had to be nearly a full-blood Were for his physical body to crumble to dust so quickly.

The only other Were I had seen die was the old woman who had shared her energy with me at my birth. She was old and her body had crumbled to dust quickly after her death. Some of the legends I had read described Were-creatures forming from energy and taking physical form at will. The Were-creatures mated with other species and became tied only to those few to whom they shared genetic bonds. The further they descended from Were-form the more the physical body, and needs, resembled those of the mortal creature. Some Were still carried more energy than mortality in their physical forms. It made shape-shifting easier.

I don't know why the creatures turned to dust. My only guess was once energy leaves a Were whatever is left of the physical is quickly consumed by the earth. Perhaps that is where the old myth of vampyres expiring in the sunlight in a poof of smoke stems from. The death of a Were causes the body to condense into dust and I could see how the puffs of grey around my black shoes might resemble clouds of smoke to the unschooled.

The priest stood by the slightly larger dust pile indicating where the cat had fallen. I could see the clouds of grey dust swirling, taking the shine off the highly polished black shoes peeking out from beneath his black pants. I could hear the screams of the raven and the fox from the woods. Whatever was chasing them must have caught up and did the same thing to them as it did to the cat. The priest turned his attention to the woods.

Whatever strange hold he had on me seemed to fade with the distraction. I turned to run, but the motion must have caught his attention because he turned and caught my eye. I couldn't move. My muscles were frozen to the point of physical pain. I could feel a fire building in my chest, filling me with rage. This priest, this *human* would not have this power over me. Darting out my tongue, I tried to taste his energy. It was there. I could taste it in the air, tingling like the flashes of lightning in a field, but his energy was hidden behind a barrier. There was a shield between me and his energy.

A flock of tiny, dark birds burst from the trees and cried out as they took off in flight. I sensed movement at the edge of the trees and struggled to find any glimpse of the creature invading my world. The wind picked up, bringing stinging motes of grit into my eyes. I didn't even have enough muscle control to blink it away. Tears formed in the corner of my eyes and trickled down my face. The priest turned from the gravesite and walked to where I was standing, immobilized by his power.

"Release me, Priest." I said the words through clinched teeth, unable to move my mouth and expel the words.

"What are you?" He asked.

He was young, probably not more than a few years older than me. Raw power emanated from the core of his being. I don't think he realized what he was doing to me. I know he didn't learn this kind of control in the seminary. The church didn't teach this any longer. Were and Vampyre creatures were considered stuff of legends. It was one of the reasons Agnes was able to so easily manipulate the people around her. It's easy to overlook something if you refuse to believe it exists.

Agnes had told me about these kinds of creatures. He was a Hunter. I didn't know much more about them except they had the power to control Were creature, but rarely had the strength to destroy us. Obviously, he was young and untrained and he didn't know what to do now that he caught me.

I reached out with my energy and tried to push against his shield, but I couldn't break free. The more I pushed the stronger he became. I stopped pushing and drew my energy inside, building it up in my body and wrapping it in a tightly contained cloak. My fingertips tingled with suppressed energy and I could feel the short hair on the nape of my neck standing on end.

The priest was standing so close to me I could smell the bacon and orange juice from his breakfast on his breath. His hand reached out but stopped short of actually touching my arm. I could feel a growl building up deep in my throat. For the first time in my life I actually felt burning hatred for my prey. His pulse was throbbing along the length of his neck and I imagined reaching out with my hands and clawing out his throat. I wanted him dead.

"Get away from it!" The deep throated order seemed to echo all around us. I narrowed in on its source, barely making out a shimmering cloud directly behind the priest.

"Show yourself!" Although the priest's voice was higher pitched, more alto than bass, his voice throbbed with authority.

The shimmering cloud pulsed and coalesced, revealing the dark form of a man. Like me and the priest, the man was dressed all in black, but it looked like he belonged to another era. His coat was long, almost cloak-like and his face was hidden in the deep folds of a hood. There was an ambiguous aura around him. It was almost as if he could have stepped into any time and place and fit right in, as if he belonged there. I could imagine him walking down the dusty streets of an old western town or standing in the crowds at the coliseum listening to the Roman senate or standing ready in a Viking ship waiting for the prow to be driven into the sand and preparing to raid a coastal city. These images flashed through my mind as if I was actually living these moments with him. The ageless quality to his face told me he probably lived all those lifetimes. I couldn't see his eyes through the folds of his cloak, but I knew he was watching me. His weapons were hidden somewhere in the energy mists swirling around his form, but I knew he had many of them on his body.

"Step away from the creature, Hunter," he commanded.

The sound of the man's voice pierced through me. I knew I was looking at my own death and I could feel the sharp pain as my muscles fought against the priest's restraining hold.

"Release me." I tried to order the priest but my voice came out as a whisper. He shrugged off my plea. His body was positioned between me and the shadow-man and he stood with his arms slightly outstretched as if to guard me.

"I will not let you harm her." He whispered too, but his voice was strong.

This priest was trying to protect me! He should be more concerned about what I would do to him once I was released from the binding holding me then he should be for my protection. I've never taken the life of an innocent, but this priest was sorely tempting me.

"It is a creature of evil." The man pushed his hood back. His face was as dark as his clothes. Dark brown, nearly black eyes stared me down. "You do not know what you protect, Hunter."

I could see the priest visibly shaking as he stood his ground. His hold on me loosened slightly and I could feel my muscles coming back under my control. I wasn't free yet and I had a feeling if I tried to move the priest would reach out and take hold of me again.

"Who are you?" Despite the shaking of his body, the priest's voice was as strong as ever.

"I am called Drakon." With a flick of his hand he gestured towards me. "I destroy that kind."

Never once did the man call me she or her. The significance was not lost on me. He did not see my human form. He saw the Were. He was a Warrior. He was my death.

Chapter Six

THE PRIEST STOOD BETWEEN Were-slayer and Were, his back straight and legs spread slightly apart as if he could survive the battle between the two. I wanted to cry out to him, to tell him to run. All hatred and anger fled from my body as I realized what he was trying to do. Most humans would have fled long before, if they would have survived this long.

The Warrior stepped forward, attempting to move past the priest, but something stopped him. Bringing his hands forward, he pushed against an invisible barrier, trying to force his way to me.

"You do not know what you protect, Hunter." His voice softened as he spoke to the priest, much like an indulgent parent would speak to a young child. "That creature will suck your soul from your body and leave you to rot like trash. It must be killed now, before it becomes too strong."

"You speak of myth and legend." An aura of blue light was growing around the priest. He was no longer shaking as he confronted the Warrior. "Why are you calling me Hunter?"

I had been wondering the same thing. It didn't seem this man of God was aware of his abilities.

"You have the aura of a Hunter." The Warrior held up his empty hands as if to assuage the priest. "I see your energy just like the Feeder does right now. You were born to the Hunter Sect, just as I was born to the Warrior Sect and it was born to the Feeders."

This was the first I had heard of Sects. I knew there were many types of Were, just as there were many races and many kinds of animals. We had evolved from the energy of the universe many millennia ago. Were-creatures were born, not made or created by some magical bite or curse. It only stood to reason that those who could hunt and kill Were could also only be born into it. I could feel the bands holding me loosen as the priest contemplated the words of the Warrior.

"I have seen things here with my own eyes I would not believe if someone told them to me," the priest said.

He took a step towards the Hunter and I felt the bands drop away completely. I stood still for a moment. His energy was still too close and I knew he could reach out and entrap me again. I had to wait for the right moment.

"Why can I see them and my brothers can't?" he asked.

My eyes followed to where he nodded and I saw two priests standing by the chapel doors. They appeared to be deep in conversation, completely oblivious to the happenings in the graveyard.

"Human eyes are blinded to the happenings of our kind." The Warrior peered through the priest and stared at me. I stood completely still. He must have satisfied himself with the thought that I was completely ensnared by the priest's power because he returned his focus to the man standing between us. "Even now, if they do see us, they will believe we are three people conversing amongst the graves. When I kill it and its body disappears into dust they will convince themselves they only saw two people in the first place."

"I will not let you take the life of this girl."

The priest was back to his defense of me. The two men squared up against each other and I decided this was my moment. I pushed myself backwards, forcing my body into a back flip covering the length of the entire graveyard. It was only after I cleared the wrought iron fence did I chance a look back. The Warrior must have tried to go through the priest to get to me because both men were on the ground in a tangle of limbs. I didn't spare a moment to think of the priest and the sacrifice he made, allowing me to escape. There was no way he could survive the encounter with the Warrior.

I ran until I was sure I wasn't being followed. I didn't look behind me or stop for anything in my path. Zigzagging my way through the city I doubled-back on my path, at times running in circles and crisscrossing the city. Wading up creeks and crossing over parks and the roof of buildings, I did everything I could to disguise my scent and throw the Warrior off my trail. Agnes had told me of the tracking power and strength of the Warriors. They were fast, but I hoped the struggle with the priest prevented him from following me. The sound of the TriMet train brought me to a stop. I had just fed a few hours before, but all the morning activity had taken a lot out of me. I needed to recharge my batteries.

The door was just sliding closed when I slipped on to the train. It was the early morning commute and the car was packed full of people headed into the heart of downtown. Affecting the relaxed facial musculature and straight ahead stare of my blind persona, I managed to grope my way to the bar in the center of the car. The train was so crowded it was easy to pass off my casual brushes and occasional bumps as accidents. I was able to draw enough energy off the train patrons to replace what I lost in this morning's confrontations. A middle-aged man arose from his seat and tapped me on the shoulder.

"Miss," he said, his voice raised slightly. "You're welcome to take my seat."

I allowed him to take my elbow and guide me to the seat he just vacated. His energy was sweet and pure and very tempting, but I only drew enough of it from him to give my body a little boost of energy. He gave my arm a gentle pat before taking my place at the center pole.

Three teenagers with long boards and windblown, shoulder-length hair boarded the train at the next stop. They stood right in front of me for the rest of ride into downtown. I stretched my leg out so every time the train rocked one of them would bump into me. The three were so involved in their animated discussion they barely noticed. I happily feasted on their energy as it bled out of their pores. They would be a little more tired than usual when they made it home tonight, but young people recover faster than adults and I knew they wouldn't feel any long-term effects from my feeding.

My senses were heightened when I exited the train and I constantly scanned the crowd as I made my way to the apartment. As I made my way down the stairs I could feel the muscles between my shoulder blades tighten like I was sensing someone staring at my back. My door was locked and it didn't look like anything was different, but I couldn't shake the feeling of being watched. As I reached to unlock the door a fluttering by the mat caught my eye. I reached down and picked up the black feather caught between the edge of the mat and the door.

Holding the feather to the light trickling down the stairs, I could see the distinct highlights of greens and blues reflecting in the shiny blackness of its surface. The feather was from a raven. The Were must have been here before they found me in the graveyard. I don't know what brought them here, but if they found me it meant my grandfather knew where I was. It also meant the Warrior could find me as well. A thrill went up my spine. I wondered what it would be like to confront the Warrior when I wasn't being held prisoner by the priest. I know the fight would be phenomenal, but I didn't think I had the skills to battle him and win. I wasn't ready, yet.

The door frame cracked as I forced the door open with one hand. I didn't even bother closing the door behind me. I wasn't going to be coming back here anyway and I knew the church would make good on any damages. Snagging my backpack, an old canvas pack I had found at a military surplus store, off the foot of the bed, I stuffed clothes and the book inside. I emptied the cupboard of every can of beans and soup and piled them on top of my small bundle of clothes. By the time I was finished the pack weighed nearly thirty pounds, but the weight was negligible compared to my strength. I thrust my arms through the straps and shrugged the pack into place. I didn't feel any sense of remorse as I exited the apartment and bounded up the stairs. I was being hunted. I could no longer afford to hole up in one place.

I needed time to think, to develop a plan. If I headed to the streets right now I would be constantly on the run. I couldn't afford the luxury of holing up in some crevice in a wall and hoping I wouldn't be found. The streets afforded the luxury of copious amounts of prey and it's pretty easy to disguise the deaths of street dwellers, but that would be my only advantage. I needed to find a rabbit-hole. Someplace where I could get lost and the Warrior would never be able to find me.

As I made my way through the streets and into back alleyways I considered my options. I could swing down by the river and hide out there. There was the camp under the Burnside Bridge. Plenty of prey lived there in semi-permanent residence. I could travel up the course of the river all the way to the ocean or inland across country. I wouldn't lack for prey and I knew there were shelters and soup kitchens where I could get food if I needed it. But, if the Warrior found me I don't know if I would be able to get away in time. The river had the resources I needed, but it would also cut off one of my means of escaping. I wasn't sure if I had the ability to jump over it and the current was unpredictable so if I tried to swim I would have no way of controlling where and when I landed on shore.

I made my way downtown. The shelter was serving breakfast so I turned in and took my place in line. Many of the regulars recognized me and shuttled me forward to the front of the line. The servers piled my tray full of eggs, biscuits, Cream of Wheat, milk and orange juice. They knew me well enough to know I wouldn't touch the bacon and sausage. I allowed one of the servers to guide me to a table. When I sat down I hunched over, curled my arm around my plate and held my spoon like a knife.

Attacking my food, I shoveled it in quickly, not allowing anyone else near me or the tray. I didn't really need to put that much effort into protecting my tray. There were enough people around who would be willing to defend the poor little blind girl from anyone who would dare take her food, but if I didn't maintain the posture others would be suspicious and I couldn't risk drawing attention to myself. I ate until I was full, not knowing when I would have my next solid meal. Food wasn't a priority for me, but I still needed to intake a few calories to keep my physical form functioning. I could run on pure energy, if I needed to, but I wanted to keep my energy in reserve for emergencies. The more calories I had to burn the less energy I would need to use.

By the time I had finished my breakfast I knew where I needed to go. If Agnes could survive there as long as she had I could surely hide out there until I could figure out my next step.

Chapter Seven

AGNES HID ME IN a section of the old convent that had been abandoned more than fifty years ago. It was easy for her to find me a bed in one of the former nun's cells. I had to store my bag under the cot in my room and my movement was limited to the three-foot strip of bare floor between the bed and the wall. It was an ideal setting for quiet reflection.

The old building with its stone walls and sweeping cathedral was magnificent. The convent was established in the early nineteenth century and had been built to accommodate nearly thirty nuns. An all-girls school was added in the early twentieth century, but with the decline of women joining convents, there was no longer enough sisters to maintain the convent and the school. The school was moved across the city and the old building was converted to a mental hospital in the middle of the century. It was in this hospital when I met Agnes and learned exactly what kind of power I had.

I was eight and I had just killed my foster father. He was a bad man, my foster father. I had only been in my new home for a few months and he hadn't done anything to me, yet. I used to huddle in my bed and listen to the other girls cry out in fear when he would sneak into their rooms. I could feel their fear creeping through the walls of the house, poisoning the air with the reek of blood and sweat.

Our foster mother was always so loaded on sleeping pills she couldn't hear our cries anyway. I think I hated her more than I hated him. No one could really be so blind and stupid to suffering under her very

47

roof. My disdain for her oozed out of my pores. She used to shudder every time she looked at me, refusing to have anything to do with my care. Most of the time the older kids looked after us, feeding us, cleaning our clothes, making sure we bathed. That was if they could bother with the younger ones. Most of the time the older kids found something to do outside of the home.

My foster-father gave me a doll for my eighth birthday. All the other children were sitting around the table staring at me. They knew what the big box meant. I tried to ignore the ugly looking creature. It had white-blond hair and big blue eyes that blinked when I tilted it. When bedtime came I left it on the couch neatly stuffed between two cushions. It didn't work. He came into my room anyway.

I tried to pretend I was sleeping. His heavy steps shuffled and stumbled across the room as he drunkenly stumbled about in the dark. My stomach still churns at the remembrance of his alcohol laced breath caressing my face as he leaned over me in my bed.

"Maria." he said. I'm sure he was trying to whisper, but his voice was harsh in my ears. "Oh, little Maria, you forgot to kiss your daddy to thank him for your present. I brought your little dolly to you."

His hands were on my shoulders, pinning me to the bed. I could feel his weight on the edge of the bed as he leaned over me. My stomach churned at the stench of his sweaty body. His mouth closed over mine and I did what came naturally to me. I was young and my powers weren't fully developed so I wasn't as efficient as I sucked his energy from his body. He struggled to pull away, but I held his head with my little hands and refused to release him until I had drained every drop of energy from his twisted, dirty soul.

His screams woke the other children, but they were too cowardly to come to my room. One of them went into the master bedroom and tried to wake our foster mom, the other two ran out the front door and down the street. One of the neighbors saw them as she was letting in her cat for the night. She's the one who called the police.

By the time my little foster brother managed to shake our foster mother from her drug induced sleep I was deep in the throes of a grand mal seizure. I was on the floor covered in vomit, both my own and my foster father's, blood, urine and feces. When I came out of the seizure all I could feel was rage. Throwing myself at the body of my foster father, I pummeled him with my fists, clawing at his face and eyes. He was dead and my rage was pointless. When my foster mother tried to pull me off him I punched her in the face, giving her a bloody nose.

The sight of her blood drew me up short. I hated her, but she was so pathetic I had no desire to hurt her. The doll was in the middle of the bed. I snatched it up and threw it on my foster father's body. When the police arrived, they found my foster mother curled over her husband's body. I was crouched on the bed snarling and growling like a wild animal.

The doctors at the hospital tried sedating me. The nurses tried strapping me down. Nothing worked. I was too strong for all of them.

Agnes was my saving grace. She had brought in a patient from the asylum and was waiting in the emergency room. When the medics dragged me, kicking and screaming, into the exam room, she recognized me for what I was and followed the doctors into the room.

No one could get near me. I was a tiny, screaming bundle of energy and as soon as a nurse approached I would strike with claws and teeth. Every person in the room had been marked by me. The doctor's face had a row of red marks, one of which was pouring a stream of bright red blood. The orderly was nursing a deep bite on his forearm and refused to come anywhere near me. There was a crowd of nurses and orderlies standing outside my room. Any time one of them would even try to enter the room I would throw whatever was closest at them. One young nurse was sprawled out in the doorway, a dent in her head from the metal bedpan I had thrown at her. The glow of her energy was fading, but someone dragged her away before she completely faded away.

When Agnes approached my bed I snarled at her, like I had the other nurses. She reached out her hand and touched my shoulder. I hissed. She gave me a gentle pat and said, "Now stop that." Her words stopped me and I dropped to the bed like a stone. The nurses and doctors were still cowering around the edges of the room, watching me with wary eyes. Agnes brushed the mane of tangled hair out of my face and peered deeply into my eyes.

"Well, there you are."

Her words were so strange, yet I felt suddenly calm as she brushed my hair and ran her hand down my frame.

"Why is this child here?" she asked.

A medic pushed himself away from the wall and moved to stand in front of Agnes. He made a strange gesture, one I felt I should recognize, and started explaining.

"She was brought in from a foster home," he said. "We think the foster father was molesting the children. We found him in her room. It looks like he died of a heart attack. The other children were brought in with her, but they seem to be normal. This one has been giving us a problem. It's like she has too much energy in her little body."

I realize now the layers of explanation he was giving Agnes. I learned later the gesture he used was one shared amongst feeders. He was saying he was one of us. Telling her it looks like my foster father died of a heart attack was his way of letting her know appearances can be deceiving and he recognized the markings of another feeder. The other children were just that: normal, human children. And finally, I had consumed too much energy and my tiny body was having problems processing it all.

Agnes stayed with me until the doctors finished. She's the one who undressed me, bathed me and changed me into clean clothes. Every gentle touch siphoned off a little extra energy, taking the burden off my body. When it was all over and the doctors determined I was perfectly healthy, physically, they released me to Agnes' care. She brought me to the asylum, the only place the doctors determined I could live and not be a risk to myself and others.

The asylum became my home. I never told Agnes my history. She knew I was powerful and began teaching me how to use my abilities, but I quickly learned how to keep secrets from her. It was hard at first because, like me, she was a mind reader, but her mind was no match for the complexity of mine.

Agnes and I were the only ones who knew the depths of the old convent and the secrets it held. She should know everything about the old building, she's lived here before the first structure was even built. I spent my childhood exploring every corner and cordoned off section of the crumbling stone corridors.

The bells rang the nine-o'clock hour. The sisters would be closeting themselves up in their cells for quiet reflection before going to bed. I had another two hours before I could leave my cell. I bided the time reading the ancient text I had brought with me from my apartment. Since meeting the Warrior in the woods I had gained a greater understanding of the original author's words. The man was chronicling the knowledge of the Warrior caste. The true depth of his knowledge was astounding.

Although the ancient chronicler didn't appear to have a great understanding of the qualities of the Were, he did know how we could be killed. As I fingered the illustrations on the page I remembered the cat's head rolling across the graveyard and its body dissolving into dust. I turned to the image of a Were-creature apparently in mid-change. A vaguely man-shaped form with an elongated snout and lips curling away from sharp teeth stared from the page. His long, grasping arms ended in claws and his legs jointed oddly, curving forward at the hips and bending at the knees like a dog's hind legs. The grotesque, hairless creature stared from the page with shining black eyes as if he was ready to leap from the pages and tear out my throat. I traced the edges of the picture with my finger, wondering what I would need to do to contort my body into the shape of this beast.

I turned my attention to the words describing the picture. It was perhaps this statement, above all others in the book that stood out most vividly in my mind.

> *The full-blooded Were is perhaps the most powerful creature known on God's Earth. He is stronger than the most powerful Warrior and can throw off any chains or binding compulsion known in the Hunter's arsenal. Beware this creature, as he can take any form. The Were are self-healing and can repair the body from any wound save a direct strike to the head or the heart. It does not take any special weaponry to kill these creatures, but any strike needs to be definite and deliberate.*
>
> *The Were have strength far beyond any human's. They can run faster, leap farther and fight longer than any ten men. It is best to come upon them by surprise or ensure you can bind them against striking when attacking.*
>
> *A Hunter with sufficient strength can take on part-blood Were but must not attempt to attack a full-blood without a Warrior or other Hunters to assist in the battle. Even with a fatal strike to a full-blooded Were, it is best to decapitate the creature to ensure death has occurred. Do not allow the Were to make physical contact with any other living Were creature in its final death throes as it can transfer its spirit to the body of the other creature, thus assuring its eternal life.*

Eternal life. Immediately the image of Agnes' worn, wrinkled face and rheumy blue eyes flashed through my mind. She once told me she's lived nearly three thousand years. Based on the topography of her face I always assumed she's lived all those years in the same body, but if this priest was correct in his assessment of the Were's ability then it was possible she has found another way to extend her life.

Chapter Eight

THE STONE WALLS ECHOED back my silence as I made my way to the library. I had returned the book to the bottom of my backpack as I contemplated what I was looking for. If Agnes had kept a book written for the Warriors she must have kept a book written for the Were. I needed to find that book.

As far as I knew I was the only one, except for Agnes, who regularly visited the library. The room existed long before the school was established, perhaps it was as old as the cathedral itself. The library was located behind strong, arching, oak doors. As I turned the handle the hinges protested. The noise wasn't loud enough to carry down the hall so I didn't bother checking back over my shoulder for anyone else in the hallways. There were always so many random noises in the building anyway I seriously doubted anyone else heard me wandering the halls.

The shelves were lined with thousands of volumes on any given subject. I wasn't really interested in the newer print books easily accessed in the front areas of the room. A thin layer of dust covered the tables and shelves blurring the titles of books and leaving trails of evidence of the passage of visitors. The shuffling tracks of footsteps created pathways through the dust to the most popular books. Fingerprints disturbed the film on the shelves and spines of books. Dust motes sparked in the air as the tiny molecules scattered when my energy disturbed them.

Only a few patients in the asylum had the wherewithal to even visit the library. A few of the nuns visited on a slightly more regular basis, especially to visit the historical texts. Occasionally one of the nurses will visit to find a book to try to relieve the monotony of their twelve-hour shift, but since the library was a carryover from the days when the building was a convent and then a school there weren't very many current publications on the shelves. From the day Agnes brought me to the musty, shelved corridors when I was eight years old I considered this library mine.

I had all night, so I wasn't in a rush. I wasn't even sure if I knew what I was looking for. The book I was carrying with me read like an instruction manual on killing Were. I figured if there was a book for Warriors there should be a book for their prey. I was tired of the lore and wanted to find out the truth about who, or what, I was. The memories I carried with me from my mother let me know who I was from her perspective. Her father was a soul-eater and could take the shape of a wolf, one of the most common Were shapes, although he had the combined genetics of more than one Were creature. Her mother was a mountain cat Were. My grandfather had captured her somewhere in the mountains of northern Utah. Were don't usually interbreed, it's just not in our mindset to consider mixing species. My great-great-grandfather, though, believed we were all descended from one genetic root and over the millennia our genes started evolving. He was trying to breed the perfect Were creature, cross-mating his genetics and those of his children to bring us back to the original antecedents. He passed this quest on to his children and grandchildren. My mother learned all this from her father when she was very young and passed this knowledge on to me when she split her soul between my body and hers.

I stepped through the dark spaces between shelves, allowing my fingers to ghost over the books. Fingering ancient volumes with crumbling spines, I allowed myself to feel the seeping age radiating from the pages. Residual energy from previous owners tickled my fingertips. Some of them seemed to vibrate with the past lives they held.

Finally deciding the books, I needed would not be found on these shelves, I turned to the last isle and moved to the alcove at the back of the room. The deep recesses of the opening were hidden in shadow, but I knew what was concealed behind its door. Removing the loose stone, a hand-span away from the bottom of the arch, I reached in and pulled out the key from its hiding place.

As I was about to insert it into the lock a noise stayed my hand. I was not alone in this quiet place. The sound of leather soled shoes on rock tiles filled the emptiness. Ducking behind a shelf, I peered out between gaps in the books. A dark form stopped on the opposite side of the shelf and turned towards me. Whatever it was moved quickly and suddenly I could see the pinpoint pupil surrounded by a blue iris staring at me through the books. I prepared myself to run, looking down the row of books for an escape route. A binding sensation overtook me and I was pinned to the spot.

"There you are."

I still couldn't make out the speaker, but I knew who it was. The priest's voice was as quiet as it was in the graveyard.

"I wondered where you got off to, child," he said. "Come out here so we can talk."

The compulsion was so strong I actually took a step, but I was able to force myself to stop. I wasn't going to let this man order me around like a marionette. I realized I still had some control over my own body, although I couldn't shake the compulsion off completely. I straightened and stared him down.

"It's all right," he said. "I'll come to you. Stay there."

His command rooted me to the spot as he shuffled his way through the dark to my hiding place. I stood stock still, unable to move as he hurried towards me. Stopping inches from where I was standing, he reached out and grabbed me by the shoulders.

"Look at you," he said. "Look at this beautiful monster."

I shook my head at the incredulity of his statement. I was anything but beautiful. In fact, the dimensions of my face were so skewed I had been told I was an ugly little creature most of my life. He pushed his face close to mine. It was obvious he was studying me.

He studied every inch of me. I realized he was young, probably in his mid-twenties. His breath smelled sweet, like fresh mint leaves. Suddenly his hands cupped my face. His fingers were warm and dry. I tried reaching into his soul to find the core of his energy, but something was blocking me from reaching him. It was like there was a shield between his soul and mine. I reached out with my mind, trying to touch his thoughts. The barrier was there as well, not as strong, but strong enough. I didn't feel any malice or hatred in his mind, only curiosity.

"Ah, yes," his voice carried with it the sibilant whisper of a lover. "Why would anyone want to destroy you?"

I knew he was not talking to me. The shine of his eyes had turned inward and he was studying me like a scientist studied a rat in the lab.

"What do you want from me?"

My words must have brought him back to the moment because he let go of my face and stepped back.

"I don't want anything from you, child." His voice was no longer a whisper. "I want to know what you are. I haven't been able to find anything about your type of creature in any book I can get my hands on and I heard the sisters here have a collection of ancient texts. I wanted to look at them. I didn't think I would find you here."

I no longer felt the binding compulsion to stay, but my curiosity was piqued. He didn't seem dangerous, so I stayed rooted to my spot.

"Why are you here so late?" I asked. "Did Sister Agnes let you in the library?"

The priest's brow wrinkled and I could almost feel his mind churning as he sought the answer to my questions.

"Is it so very late?" His mind seemed clouded as if it was lost in a fog. I sent a probing burst of energy into his mind, but it didn't penetrate beyond the mist. "I must have lost track of time. No, Sister Agnes didn't let me in. I wanted to explore the library, so I came here. Things are a little different for me since I met you, child. I'm not experiencing the world the way I used to."

"I wish you would stop calling me child." I said it without anger or malice. Now that he no longer held me bound to him I had no reason to hate.

"I'm sorry," he sounded sincere in his apology. "It must just be habit from my training. I am…I mean I was training to be a priest. We call everyone child. What is your name?"

"Maria Christine." I saw no harm in giving him my name. It really didn't mean anything to me anyway.

"Ah, a beautiful name to go with a beautiful creature."

Again, I didn't understand the beautiful reference. I knew I was so small and skinny many people mistook me for a young boy. My face was asymmetrical, not lending itself to any image of traditional beauty. Nondescript, sandy-brown hair blended with the slightly pale caste to my skin. I was anything but beautiful.

"Who are you?"

This was the first time I noticed he wasn't dressed in the traditional priest's garb. In fact, if anything he was dressed exactly like I was, black pants, black shirt, black shoes. He was as nondescript as I was.

"I was going to be Father Conner," he smiled depreciatingly. "Now I think I'm going to need to go back to my given name. I am Andrew and I think I belong to you now."

My heart throbbed in my chest. I could feel my blood pounding through my veins. I didn't like this man. Every part of my being cried out to run. Yet, as

I moved to run I felt an overwhelming compulsion to stay. He no longer held me. All I had to do was command my feet to move and I would be out of the library in seconds. I knew I could outrun him. I finally gathered enough will to step back, but as I moved he reached and grabbed my arm.

"Don't leave," his voice was gentle and calm. I could feel the warmth of his hand against my arm, but his fingers weren't exerting any pressure against my skin.

"What do you want from me?"

He drew close to me again, putting his face close to mine he breathed the words. "I want to know what's going on. Something happened in that graveyard, something my books can't explain. I need to know."

The sound of the doors creaking open broke the tension of the moment. Andrew dropped his hand off my arm and stepped back into the shadows. Making a quick motion with his hand he made it known I wasn't to say anything. I pulled myself up straight and tried to shake off the last of the daze I was feeling. By the time I came back to myself Andrew had disappeared somewhere beyond the shelves of the library. I could hear shuffling footsteps approaching so I moved to meet Agnes as she made her way to the back of the room.

Chapter Nine

I MOVED FROM MY hiding place amongst the books and was waiting for her when she came around the corner and approached the door to the locked office. She smiled as she shuffled her way to me.

"I thought I heard voices back here. Were you talking to yourself?" Agnes patted my arm and brushed past me to get to the door. I held out the key to her.

"I was looking for more books on the Were-creatures." I didn't answer her question, letting her think I had reverted to my childhood habit of talking to myself. If she couldn't sense the presence of the priest, no wait, he wasn't a priest any longer, if she couldn't sense the presence of Andrew, I didn't need to be the one to tell her about him.

Agnes unlocked the sturdy, wooden door and placed the key back in its hiding place. I never really thought the hiding place was that great, but since no one really delved too deeply into the library it was a safe enough place. Before she walked into the room Agnes flipped the light switch, flooding the small, musty office with bright yellow light. I took a moment to allow my sight to adjust to the change of light. I hadn't bothered turning on the libraries overhead lights relying on my own unique vision to find my way around. Agnes had brought a flashlight with her and as she entered the office she clicked it off, placing it on the desk as she made her way to the office chair. She obviously couldn't see as well as I could in the dark. I followed her into the office, not bothering to sit down. I rarely sat, my body was always too energized to stay still for very long and I tended to fidget if I stayed in one place too long.

I watched as Agnes took a slender silver key out of the pocket of her robe. She slid the key into the lock of one of the desk drawers and pulled it open. A scattering of yellowing papers filled the depths of the drawer. Agnes shuffled through the papers, pushing them aside to reveal the wooden bottom of the drawer. Pushing against the wood until it clicked, she slid aside the panel, revealing a tiny niche. She withdrew the slim, black, leather-bound volume hidden within the recess of the drawer and handed it to me. I could feel the weight of the contents of the book as she transferred ownership to me. I flipped it open and scanned the words scrawled across the page. It was written in a scrawling hand in a strange language. By the third sentence I was able to decipher the language as being Old English. It wasn't my favorite language to read, especially since the spelling of many English words weren't consistent until the late fifteenth century, but I could at least understand the flow of the contents.

"It's a journal of a young Anglo-Saxon girl." Agnes said. "I found her in a village in lower Brittany. She was the only survivor of a raid. Even in her broken state I could feel the power in her soul. We took up residence in an old stone cottage. I taught her how to write as I taught her how to use her other powers. It wasn't until a few months later I realized she was with child, the result of the rape of Norman soldiers." Agnes paused as I thumbed through the journal.

"You won't find any mention of the child in the journal." Agnes said after a few minutes. "She didn't show much interest in the boy, even when she was pregnant with him. She died when he was barely two. I took care of him, taught him how to feed, brought him wives. The girls weren't important. I was more interested in the children they produced." Her eyes took on a distant look and she smiled at the remembrance. "There are descendants of my little foundling all over the world. I don't even know if I can trace them all. As far as I know you could be one of them."

I traced the spidery handwriting on the pages as Agnes explained the source of the work to me. "She was young, but by her writing shows wisdom beyond her age. You might learn a few things from her."

"How long did you stay with the family?" I asked.

"Oh, I became bored after a few generations." Agnes gave me a misty smile. "I don't have the patience to deal with children. Most Were don't show their promise until puberty and while I'm waiting for their talent to manifest I must put up with dozens of whiney brats. It was a lot of work for an occasional flash of brilliance."

I tucked the book in the pocket of my sweatshirt. I wondered if Agnes wanted the copy of the priest's book back now that I had this one, but she didn't say anything and as long as she wasn't going to bring it up I would just leave it in my backpack.

I ran my fingers through my hair, making the short spikes stand on end. When I showed up at the convent Sophia took one look at my badly shorn head and sat me down, attacking the unevenly cropped locks with a pair of scissors. The result was a very short, but even, cut making me look more boyish than ever. It would take a while for my hair to grow to an unmanageable length again but I still considered snagging Sophia's scissors from her and tucking them in my backpack, but I wanted to wait until I decided to leave. The nuns tend to get nervous when sharp objects disappear around mental patients.

I moved towards the door, but Agnes stood up and moved in front of me, preventing me from leaving.

"You're leaving soon."

It was a statement, not a question. There wasn't any point in trying to keep secrets from Agnes. She knew me almost as well as I knew myself. I learned how to close Agnes out of my mind a long time ago, but she could still predict my behavior and guess my next move.

"In the next night or two." I rubbed my hand against the journal, wondering if Agnes would want it back now. "I need to feed so I have enough energy, but I'm thinking of heading south. I could go to California or Nevada, there's enough prey there and I wouldn't have to worry about extreme weather. I wouldn't have to bother with shelter."

Agnes nodded. I'm sure she spent enough of her life running from Hunters and she knew exactly what I was running from.

"Before you go, I need your help with a task." She moved away from the door, knowing I wouldn't try to leave before she was done talking. "Gather as much energy as you can tonight. Meet me in Sophia's chambers tomorrow at midnight. You can leave when we are finished."

I nodded my understanding. I could see the pain Sophia was carrying with her as she tried to push herself through each day and I knew whatever Agnes was planning would relieve the suffering of the young nun.

Before I returned to my chambers I stopped by the kitchen and grabbed a couple cans of soup from the pantry. Once I returned to my tiny cell I stuffed the book into the bottom of my backpack with the other one and piled my clothes on top. There wasn't very much room left for the cans of food, so I stacked them in a pile underneath the bed.

The metal bed frame held the mattress off the ground a few inches, allowing me to stack the cans a few deep. I had collected a few more from the asylum kitchens, sneaking in after the kitchen was shut down for the night. Stretching out full length on the floor, I studied the shiny metal reflecting through the dust motes. Big gallon tins of hominy, small twelve-ounce cans of soup. All the food I would need to keep my physical body alive for months. For most humans this amount of food would last a week, maybe two if they restricted calories, but for me, well, I would last months on this collection. As long as I had my other energy source.

Thinking about the food made me deeply aware of the burning hunger in my gut. I pushed myself up from my prone position and moved to the door. A flash of movement caught my eye and I turned. For a moment I thought I saw a shadow of a figure, but when I gazed into the corner nothing was there. I focused my gaze, trying to force the image back into my sensory perception, but it was gone. It must have just been a shadow cast by the light of the moon streaming in the narrow window enclosure.

I wasn't planning to hunt right away so I settled into the thin mattress and read the journal. The girl was very simple and most of her story centered on her hatred of the soldiers responsible for killing her family and leaving her pregnant and alone. It wasn't a riveting read and I soon became bored with her whining. I finished reading the journal in just a few hours and decided to go ahead and hunt now instead of waiting another day.

As I left the room I thought I heard a sigh, but I refused to turn around. There was no way anyone else could have been in my room. The rectangular shaped room didn't have any closets or cubbyholes and there wasn't room under the bed for anyone to hide. I closed the door and made my way down the hall to the asylum.

No other souls stirred in the hallways as I made my way to the hospital wing of the convent. It wasn't surprising since the building once meant to house over a hundred nuns and nearly a thousand students now only housed one small mental hospital. Most of the nuns resided in the far wing of the convent. There were only ten other sisters residing in the actual cloistered section of the building. Agnes and Sophia saw to the day to day operations of the convent, overseeing the nuns in their work, providing service to the community and overseeing the needs of the hospital. The cloistered nuns worked at the hospital, but there weren't enough of them to staff the entire facility. I knew I would have to work my way around the nurses and aides working the night shift to find an energy source to feast upon.

I supposed I could have fed on one of the hospital staff, making it look like an attack by one of the patients. There were enough violent offenders in the ward I could have easily made it look like one of them got the jump on a nurse and killed her, but most of the staffers here were compassionate nurses just trying to help the less fortunate. One or two of them were self-serving bitches just putting their hours in on the job, but they were harmless. None of them were feeders, Agnes wouldn't tolerate the competition for her food source.

There were a hundred and one patients in the mental hospital. Some of them were just in for short term evaluation and medicine adjustments, but most of them were permanent residents. They were brought here by families frustrated and unable to care for the needs of a seriously ill individual or ordered here by the court because they were deemed too crazy to stand trial for their crimes. There was nowhere else for these forgotten souls except for this dark place. Even the ones cared for by their families were eventually forgotten and visits from their loved ones slowly came to a stop. There was no one who really cared about their welfare. No one to know whether they lived or died.

I made my way down the hall towards the locked door separating the convent from the asylum. Stopping at the large, wooden obstacle, I reached into the pocket of my hoodie and pulled out the key Agnes had given me when I came to her and requested sanctuary. I guess sanctuary isn't exactly the right term for what I requested, but it's the closest approximation to my reasons for hiding out in the convent.

I slid the key into the lock and listened at the door for a moment. No sound penetrated the darkness and I couldn't feel any waves of residual energy in the void beyond the door. Turning the key in the lock, I could hear the tumblers slide and click. Agnes always kept this door well-oiled and the heavy door opened with barely any creaking sound. Opening the door only wide enough to slide my body through, I oozed my way into the asylum and closed and locked the door behind me. Slipping the key back into my pocket of my sweatshirt, I prepared myself for the hunt.

Chapter Ten

MY TARGET WAS JUST beyond the nurse's station at the end of a long hallway. I drew my energy into myself, forcing it into a tiny ball in the center of my chest. I needed to be careful not to overextend myself since I barely had enough contained energy for this hunt. I placed my hand on the wall, feeling its rough, uneven surface, imperceptible to the human eye. My fingers gripped the wall and I found easy purchase. Climbing up the wall, I positioned myself at the joint between the wall and the ceiling. The only bright lights were above the nurse's station. The rest of the hall lights were turned down low and I was able to hide in the shadows as I crept to the ceiling.

I made my form as small as possible as I inched my way down the hall. A little nurse's aide was just entering a room as I neared her. She stopped for a moment, glanced around and shuddered. I stayed completely still until she entered the room and then continued on my way.

I sped along the ceiling, easily passing the nurses without being noticed, and made my way to the room I was looking for. I could feel the throbbing presence of raw, untapped energy bleeding from the room's occupant. He literally oozed power. Opening the door, I stepped across the threshold to the white-walled room. All sound was absorbed by the padding lining the floors, wall and ceiling. The room's lone occupant was huddled against the wall, bundled in the white, heavily buckled jacket restraining his arms. As I stepped into the room he rolled on his side and glared at me. His pupils were so dilated I couldn't even tell the color of his eyes. He could see me, though. Pulling himself up as much as he could, he gave me a gaping, leering grin. A strangled sound erupted from his chest and I realized he was laughing at me. The laughter turned into choking sob. His eyes glazed over and rolled back in his head.

His energy was tainted by the anti-psychotic drugs in his system. I could taste the bitterness of the drugs flashing through the green aura of his life-force. As I crept towards him his glazed eyes slowly began to focus and he looked at me again. His eyes widened and his mouth gaped open with a silent scream. I could feel the horror oozing out of his pores and he kicked his heels into the white padding on the floor, trying to push himself farther into the corner. Reaching for his jacket, I used the stiff, cotton fibers to pull his body to the floor. He was young and strong, stronger than any one I had ever fed on before

As I brought my mouth towards his he turned his face away. Grunts and groans sounded in his throat and he arched his body from the floor. I pressed my body against his, forcing him to lie still. He struggled against me, trying to use his chest and hips to buck me off my perch. I sat on his hips and used my weight to grind him into the ground. I grabbed his hair with my hands, twisting the roots until he groaned in pain. I was so much stronger than he could ever be.

Putting my face close to his, I turned his head so he was looking at me again. "I'm giving you as much as a chance as you did those families." I growled out the words from between clenched teeth.

I could see the fear in his eyes as he realized why I chose him. I was his own personal Hellish demon coming to wreak vengeance for the families he killed. His mouth gaped and I brought my face even closer to his. Drool oozed out of his gaping maw and rolled down his chin. I shuddered and pulled my mouth away. I needed to drain him quickly, but the thought of putting my mouth on his churned what little food I had in my stomach. There are places on the body where energy seeps out and it's easy to tap into the stream. The mouth is the easiest, expelling life with every breath, but there are other places nearly as effective to draw the soul out of the body. I pushed the man's head back and placed my mouth over the throbbing, pulsating point below his chin.

I could taste his fear, even through the mind-numbing narcotics flowing through his veins. His energy was bitter, almost noxious in its flavor. His energy flowed from his essence into mine and the rhythm of his pulse sped up as he fought me. His body flopped like a fish pulled out of the water, writhing and gasping for air and hope. I slowed my feeding, savoring his horror as I pulled his life from his core.

His pulse fluttered against my lips and then slowly fade into nothingness. He arched one last time then his body stopped fighting and began to stiffen. Pulling my mouth from his neck I surveyed the wreck of his body. His face was contorted into a masque of pain and horror and his limbs were disarticulated and twisted into grotesque angles. A huge, red welt was rising in relief of the whiteness of his neck and two beads of bright red blood had welled at the surface where my teeth had pierced his skin. I didn't taste his blood in my mouth so he must have just started bleeding. Since his heart had stopped I knew there wouldn't be any more blood springing to the surface, but the mark of my mouth against his skin was unmistakable. I loosened one of the straps on his strait-jacket and wrapped the long white band around his neck, pulling it as tight as I could. The markings from the band would disguise the feeder bruise on his neck, at least from those who didn't know what to look for on the bodies. I knew his death wouldn't be investigated too deeply and the families of the seventeen victims of his rampages would finally have closure. Three years was long enough to escape impunity for the slaughter of innocents.

I could feel the toxicity from the drugs as I filtered his energy. My body tensed as I tried to force the poison out through my pores. I don't sweat. The only function of my pores is to expel bad energy as I separated it from the good. I had wanted to get out of the room and into the empty wings of the convent before the seizures took over my body, but I could already feel the twitching in my right eye.

I did my best to position the body of the man so he was facing away from the door, curled into a position that at least looked like he was sleeping. Crawling to the wall beside the door, I positioned myself out of sight-line of the window. Just in time, because I could feel the fog creep over my mind and the aching tension in my muscles as the seizure took control of my body.

The seizure didn't last long. They never do. I could feel the ache in my muscles and the wave of exhaustion flow over my body. I stayed perfectly still, waiting for the good energy to kick in and allow my body to reboot. As I slowly came back to myself I became aware of the sensation of being watched. It wasn't one of the aides or nurses, all their energy was concentrate at the other end of the building. I opened my eyes and peered around the room, looking for the being daring to watch me in my most vulnerable moments.

A dark form coalesced in the corner and started to move towards me. I blinked rapidly, trying to force the form into some semblance of human shape. It took a moment, but the image of the priest finally took shape. He crouched over me and slowly brought his hand to my face.

"What are you doing here?" I hissed at him as I sat up and pushed myself away from his outstretched hand.

The priest looked from me to the huddled form against the far wall of the room. He reached his hand out in a silent gesture to aid me from the floor, but I refused the offer. Scrambling to my feet, I pressed my body into the padding on the wall.

"Why are you here, Priest?" I wanted to press him for an answer. "Are you following me? What do you want from me?"

The priest remained silent. He dropped his hand, but his eyes still studied me as if trying to see beneath my skin and reveal my soul. I inched towards the door, hoping he wouldn't follow. So far, he seemed rooted to the spot, following me only with his eyes. I thought about attacking him, but I remember how soundly he was able to hold me during our confrontation with the Warrior and I didn't want to take the chance of him being able to control me again.

I had closed the door when I entered but hadn't allowed it to latch knowing there was no door handle on the inside. I suppose I could have climbed to the ceiling and make my way into the crawlspace above the room, but I really didn't relish the idea of having to make my escape through the ceiling tiles, not with all the layers of muck and dust piled up after years of neglect. Prying the door open, I steadied myself against the doorframe for a moment before crawling my way up the walls to begin my journey back to my room. The priest watched me go but didn't try to stop me.

I eased my way down the darkened hallways, keeping to the shadows. Instead of turning towards the entrance of the cloistered section of the convent I headed to the main kitchen at the far end of the building. Slipping through the swinging doors, I made my way to the pantry. I snagged a can of peaches and a can of corn from the shelves before I headed to the door at the back of the kitchen. The door was locked, as usual, but I had the master key, so escaping into the convent was quick and easy.

The weight of the canned food pulled at the pocket in front of my sweatshirt. It was oddly comforting to know I had more food to add to my collection. I was going to need to find a bigger backpack if I was going to bring all my stored food with me when I left. As I made my way through the empty corridors of the convent I contemplated the dilemma in the back of my mind.

My cell was cold and dark when I entered. I moved to place my cans of food under the bed without bothering with the light. I could see well enough without it. Pulling the cans out of my sweatshirt, I crouched to place them with the others. It took me a moment to realize something was wrong. All of my cans of food were missing. I groped around the grim and the dust searching for any stray cans, but they were all gone. I searched the room. It didn't take long since the room was small and only contained the bed. My backpack was missing as well as the food.

Cramming my two remaining cans into the pocket of my sweatshirt, I rushed from my room and hurried down the hall. There were only two people who knew I was in the convent and Sister Sophia was too weak to carry my cans out of my room. I needed to find Agnes.

I slowed my pace as I approached the occupied wing of the convent. Most of the nuns were sleeping. I could feel their energy ebbing and flowing with each inhalation and exhalation of breath. Sister Sophia was awake. Her anguish was overwhelming as waves of pain ate away at her hip. There was no way she would have had the physical strength and endurance to carry my food away. Agnes had been sapping her energy away in slow, deliberate feedings and with each feeding the cancer spread even further. It wouldn't have been as bad for Sophia if she wasn't also part Were. I could barely read her Were energy, but it was there, lying dormant in her soul.

I sent out probing energy spikes, looking for Agnes. She wasn't in her own cell. It only took me a few more seconds to find her since I was pretty sure I knew where she would be. Agnes was at Sophia's bedside, gentle brushing her fingers against the side of her face, sapping the young woman's energy from her body. The image was burned in my mind despite the thick walls separating us. I sent a thought to Agnes, letting her know I was waiting for her.

Hidden in a dark recess, I buried myself in the darkness as I waited for her. I didn't have to wait long. Her probing thoughts invaded my mind. I could feel her rooting around in my emotions, trying to figure out why I had ventured into the occupied section of the convent. I could almost hear her chuckle when she saw the emptiness I had found under my bed. Agnes called me to her and I left my hiding place, moving towards Sophia's room.

Chapter Eleven

SOPHIA DIDN'T EVEN REACT when I opened the door and stepped into her dimly lit cell. Both women were kneeling, shoulder to shoulder, beside Sophia's narrow bed. Agnes must have helped her out of bed. They were holding Rosaries and the beads were sliding through their fingers as whispered words dripped off their lips. Sophia slumped and nearly fell over when Agnes moved away from her, creating a neat little gap between the two of them. The hollow words of the prayer never stopped as Agnes motioned for me to kneel between them. I don't know what she expected from me, I didn't pray. I had no use for a God who could create soul-sucking monsters hell-bent on feeding on humans no matter how much suffering they caused. Just because I was one of those creatures it still didn't justify my existence.

The words Sophia whispered through her bluing lips were barely audible. I could hear the name of the Holy Mother above everything else. Sophia choked the words out through pain-filled gasps. Every breath was an effort. Each throb of her heart-beat weaker. Her eyes opened a crack and she peered at me with glazed eyes as if she was pleading for relief.

"We must hurry." Agnes' whisper seemed so loud in the heavy atmosphere of the room. "I wasn't planning on doing this tonight. I wanted to give you time to read the journal, but I need you now."

I had read the journal, but the ancient language was so twisted I wasn't sure how much of it I understood. Sophia slumped against the bed, but she struggled back to her knees. The whispered prayers never stopped.

The journal. The girl had a limited understanding of the world, but her scribbled words described being saved from a brutal attack by a woman who could have only been Agnes. She talked about learning to avenge her attack and how she would sacrifice even her own life for the sake of her savior. Even giving up her body so the old woman could live wouldn't be much of a sacrifice. Suddenly I knew what I needed to do.

Wrapping my arms around the frail body of the suffering woman, I brought my mouth to hers. Her life's energy fairly leaped from her body into mine. Her labored breathing stilled and her heartbeat quivered to a stop. I let go of her body, allowing the now limp form to sag into the bed.

Agnes suddenly grabbed my head and brought her lips down on mine. I could feel her fingernails cutting into my flesh and her mouth was pressed so hard into mine my teeth were cutting into my bottom lip. I was so startled by the force of the energy pouring into my body I nearly lost consciousness. A sudden voice inside my head called out to me and brought me back to myself. I pushed hard against Agnes' body, forcing her away from me. Her fingernails scraped against my flesh and I could feel the sting of open wounds on my cheeks and the drip of warm blood streaming down my face.

My whole body tingled from the pent-up energy Agnes had forced into me. I could feel the burning of her soul against the very nerves of my body. Pain wracked every inch of my skin and I could feel the churning of my stomach protesting the little bit of food

I had eaten that day. I felt like I was coming apart at the seams. Stumbling, I fell across the bed and knocked Sophia's body to the floor. On instinct I reached down to catch the body. My hand missed her arm and seemed to land on its own accord on her chest, just above her heart. An electric shock went through me and I lost all ability to move. Whatever Agnes had forced in to me was pouring out through the connection between my hand and Sophia's body.

I could feel Agnes inside of me. Her energy was like giant tentacles, wrapping around my heart and brain and soul. She was pulling at me, dragging my energy from my body, trying to take me with her. I fought. It was hard, so hard. She was strong and I could feel myself giving in to her.

Sophia's body twitched and shuddered under my hand and I could feel her heart start to beat again. The grayness faded from her cheeks and her skin was slowly starting to turn pink. Her chest suddenly expanded with a gasp of air and her eyes flew open. It wasn't Sophia looking out at me from behind her blue eyes. I could see Agnes' soul reflecting back at me. The old soul-eater had taken possession of the young nun's body. Agnes grabbed my hand and pinned it down on her chest.

"Now I will take you, child." Agnes' smile on Sophia's face made me shudder. "Your energy will make me the most powerful soul-eater in history."

I tried to wrench my hand from her grasp, but she had a tight hold on me. A hold that went beyond just physical entrapment. Her energy was wrapped so tightly around mine I couldn't break free.

"No!" A sudden cry out of the darkness forced Agnes to break her hold on me. "Let her go!"

I tried to push myself up from the floor, but my body protested and my stomach contents made a sudden appearance, splashing with great force against the still form of Sophia's now possessed body. My last conscious image was of the priest standing over the top of me watching as I lost myself to the seizures.

There was a different quality to the light as I drifted back to awareness. It was still dark, but everything had a soft, silver glow to it. I realize I was outside and the light source was the moonlight filtering through the trees. I don't remember leaving the confines of the convent, but somehow I ended up in this strange copse of trees. My body felt as if it had been hit by a thousand hammers. Every movement brought sharp pain and popping of my ligaments. I staggered to my feet and stood, waiting for the world to stop spinning and settle into place.

The skin on my face felt tight and sticky. When I brushed my hands against my face they came away sticky and wet, darkened with rich, nearly purple blood. Seeing my own blood was a new experience for me. I was rarely injured since I was stronger and less fragile than humans and it usually took great force to damage my skin. Agnes was much stronger than her fragile looking body appeared.

I could hear the gurgling sound of running water nearby, so I turned toward it. As I slowly made my way over the uneven ground towards a small stream I realized I was at the bottom of a deep ravine. I could see the lights of the city above me, so I knew I couldn't have traveled too far.

The stream was a shallow trickle of water, but it was cool and clear. I scooped a handful of water and used my hands to scrub the drying blood off my face.

Using the sleeve of my sweatshirt, I blotted my face dry. I didn't have a mirror to check the condition of my face, so I brushed my fingers over the surface of my skin to see if I could feel any anomalies. My face felt smooth and clean. I couldn't even feel any rough patches where Agnes' fingernails had clawed their way across my cheeks. Whatever damage she had done had healed over and my face felt smooth again.

I wanted to look in a mirror and make sure I got all the blood, but my pack with all my supplies was back at the convent. It was too dangerous to go back there, I realized the danger now. Agnes didn't save me from myself because she wanted to teach me how to be a feeder. She saved me so she could feed on my soul and become stronger.

Agnes intended to suck my soul. I knew feeders could suck the souls of other feeders. It's just more difficult to break through the natural barriers we've built around our energy. Agnes knew my defenses, she's the one who taught me how to shield my energy from other feeders. She knew I would be vulnerable during the transfer of her energy to Sophia's body. Her entire goal was to drag me from my form into Sophia's where she could keep my energy trapped and feast on me forever.

Agnes had locked part of her mind away all those years she had been caring for me and teaching me how to feed. She was a true Succubus, unfeeling, uncaring, living only for herself. She could have taught Sophia how to feed. Sophia was in my head now, I understood her history. If she had learned to tap into her power she could have cured her bone cancer, instead the woman suffered and wasted away until she was too sick to take care of herself. Sophia was descended from feeders. She had to have been for Agnes to take over her body. Feeders are as close to human as any creature can be, but somehow there was a mutation in our genomes allowing us to bend energy and manipulate matter. Sophia didn't know she was a feeder because Agnes had taken her away from her family when she was an infant. She had raised her to become the next vessel to host her soul. Agnes had been feeding on Sophia from the time she was a small child.

I sat on a large, flat rock contemplating my next move. I couldn't go back to the convent, Agnes would be waiting for me. I wondered if I should stop calling her Agnes and start referring to her as Sophia. She would take the name along with the persona when she revealed her miracle to the Bishop. I saw it happening just as Agnes planned it. Sophia would call the Bishop to the cell where Agnes' body was sprawled on the floor. She would tell how she was kneeling in prayer, pleading for healing when Sister Agnes came to her saying God revealed Sophia's pain to her and said if she was willing to sacrifice her life for her, Sophia could be healed. Agnes gave Sophia her own Rosary and then collapsed and died. Sophia would say as soon as Agnes died all the pain in her leg went away and she could walk and run as if she were a little girl again. A miracle of healing at the hands of a self-sacrificing Sister, the first step on the road to sainthood.

My hands were pale white against the moonlight. Their pristine, delicate whiteness of my skin belied my strength. I could wrestle lions and bears and come off the victor, I was sure of it. I rubbed my hands against my face. It felt clean and smooth. I didn't sweat, my body didn't secrete oil and my skin didn't dry out. I didn't get dirty or stinky because there was nothing for muck to bond to like it did with humans.

My clothes felt grimy against my skin. I had been wearing the sweatshirt and jeans for a couple of days and they had both accumulated dirt and other stains. Unlike my skin, the cloth absorbed dirt and grime from the streets. Thinking about the state of my clothing reminded me my pack was still at the convent. My pack contained my change of clothes as well as the books Agnes had given me. I really didn't care all that much about the clothes, I just wished I had the books. There was still more information I could glean from them.

The sky was beginning to brighten, foretelling the rising of the sun. It was going to be a bright, clear day. People would be out in the parks, walking around downtown, basically spending as much time in the sunshine as possible. They would practically be oozing energy and I couldn't risk exposing myself to the crowd because Agnes would be looking for me. She knew the streets as well as I did and would have no problems locking on to my energy signature. I needed to leave Portland and find a place where I could bury my energy signature, at least until I learned to hide it from Agnes.

"Shouldn't you be finding a safe place out of the sun?"

The question came from a clump of trees to my left. I leaped to my feet and turned to face my antagonist. The priest was standing, half hidden, in a clump of trees. Most of his face was hidden in shadow, but I had no doubt it was him.

Chapter Twelve

HE SEEMED TO BE everywhere and nowhere all at once. I shifted position, trying to assess the best angle to attack him. His eyes followed my movements, but he didn't move from where he was standing, or leaning. He was leaning against a tree, his arms crossed as if he didn't have anything to worry about.

"Won't you burst into flame or turn into dust when the sun's rays hit you?"

His voice had a slight uplifting lilt to it as he asked the question. I couldn't tell if he was seriously asking me if I would be destroyed by the sun's rays or if he was joking. He wasn't afraid of me. This surprised me. Just about every person I have ever had any contact with has been terrified of me.

"Why don't you leave me alone, Priest?" I fairly spit the last words out at him. He still didn't move from his spot.

"I'm not a priest." His voice seemed heavy, lower than I remembered. "Call me Andrew, that was my name before all of this happened."

I wasn't sure what he meant by his statement. I guess finding out there are such things as monsters under the bed and things that go bump in the night is enough to shake up your world view.

"The sun's going to be up soon." He adjusted his position slightly, dropping his arms and moving away from the tree. "Don't you need to be somewhere dark?"

I almost laughed out loud, but stopped myself just in time.

"I won't disappear in a puff of smoke if that's what you're worried about." The gulch wasn't very deep and I had already spotted a way up to level ground. I needed to find somewhere less exposed and figure out my next plan of attack. The past two days taught me I wasn't safe in Portland any longer. I needed to gather supplies and get away.

As I turned to move towards the trail the priest called out to me. I stopped and reluctantly turned back to see what he wanted. At first, I couldn't spot him, but after a moment I saw him emerging from the trees. He was carrying a familiar pack in his hands.

"Agnes brought your pack to this gulch." He held the pack towards me, but when I didn't move to take it he dropped it at his feet. "I watched her pack it full of your stuff. She even put in a bunch of canned food, but she returned most of your collection to the kitchens."

I didn't move to my pack until he took a few steps back into the trees. When I felt it was safe I leapt forward grabbed the pack and returned to the foot of the trail. All of this was accomplished so fast the priest didn't even have time to blink. I flipped the pack open and rummaged through the contents. All my clothes and food I had packed before going to the convent were still there, along with my cell phone, which was dead as a rock. I dug to the bottom of the pack searching, but I knew even before I got to the bottom, my books were missing. Everything was a tangled mess and out of order. I would have never packed my stuff like this. Turning the bag over, I dumped the contents on the ground and sorted them into neat piles, shaking out the clothes and folding them as I went. The books were not in my bag.

"She took the books." The priest hadn't moved from his spot. "She left everything else, but she took the books. I don't know what her plans were, but I watched her bring the bag to this gulch and leave it here in the bushes. I think she was planning on bringing you here when she was finished with you."

When she was finished with me. I knew what he meant. I wasn't supposed to survive the soul transfer. Agnes, now in the strong, healthy body of Sophia, was planning on bringing my body, or somebody resembling me if mine crumbled to dust, to this gulch and leave it exposed to the elements. I would have just been another transient victim of some random act of violence. Just another flash in the pan, a victim of the culture.

I looked down at the piles at my feet. Two changes of clothes, six pair of underwear, a cell phone, seven random cans of food, a pair of shoes, two tank tops. I didn't wear a bra. I never developed enough in that area to need one. These items piled on the ground were the essence of my life.

I'm surprised Agnes didn't complete the illusion by adding soap and feminine products to the mix. I rarely entered menses since I was barely developing into my adult phase but I was usually prepared just in case and I guess since Agnes stopped cycling herself she forgot I was just entering my cycle of fertility. Maybe she'll realize her mistake once Sophia's body entered menses.

He was still watching me as I repacked everything into the pack. The cans of food went on the bottom in a tiny little stack. Rolling up my spare hoodie, I stuffed it between the cans and where the pack would rest against my back. It only took a few moments to repack the bag. I hefted it over my shoulders and buckled the straps against my chest. I tried to ignore him for the few seconds it took me to get my bag packed, but he seemed to be omnipresent. His eyes tracked me as I adjusted the pack and prepared to head up the trail. I could feel his eyes burning into the back of my head as I took the first few steps up the trail.

"Don't go," he whispered.

His voice was soft, pleading and I almost turned, but my feet were headed up and I didn't want to stop my forward motion. I had to get out of Portland. I had to get as far away from Agnes and my grandfather as I could.

"I know what you are." He called after me. "You don't scare me."

I turned. He was still hidden under the trees so I moved back down the trail and sat down on my rock. The sun was just rising over the horizon and a beam of light filtered down, warming my body. I automatically turned my face to capture its energy.

"So beautiful"

It was whispered, but I still heard him. I turned back to find him in the shadows. It took me a while. He had retreated farther back into the copse of trees.

"You're a creeper." I narrowed my eyes and stared at him. Watching to see if he would move closer.

"I'm not…" he struggled with his words. "I don't think of you that way."

I could see he was telling the truth. The great thing about being a Were, we don't release pheromones unless we're in heat. Sexual attraction required at least some form of pheromone exchange.

"Why are you following me?" I had to know why I couldn't shake him. Humans were my prey. I wasn't used to trying to hide from my main food source.

"I'm not following you." He stepped closer, nearly out of the shadows. I could make out his form, but his face was still hidden. "You're just everywhere I go. I think we are meant to be together. I'm called to you. I don't know why I can't stop…"

I stood up suddenly and he started, moving farther back into the trees. It was too soon. He had information I needed. Well, maybe not needed, but I wanted to know what he knew. I sat back down and waited. I didn't have to wait for long.

"The creatures in the cemetery," he said. "I thought they were creatures of legends. I read all the books. I know the histories. There are things they don't teach us in school, or in the seminary, but I know they're out there." He turned and looked into the trees. "I know Agnes. She raised me, like she did Sophia. We were in the orphanage together. She used to tell us stories about living in Germany and Ireland and America. But they weren't stories of her life, they were stories of living through raids of Germanic tribes and witch trials. It thought they were just stories, but I think she was telling the truth. She lived through every story she told me."

I sat as silent as the stone under me, absorbing all the priest said. I knew Agnes was ancient, but I hadn't thought about how she obtained her immortality. The human body lives about seventy years, give or take, as long as it does not sustain injury or get a disease. The Were, well, the Were can live to be hundreds of years by all the reckoning I could discover. Of course, our ability to age is dependent on the ratio of Were DNA compared to human DNA in our genetic makeup. There isn't any purebred Were in existence. At least, Agnes always told me there weren't any purebreds left. The Were strain was becoming so diluted it was difficult to find those with the capability to consume the entire energy of a human by themselves. Perhaps it was for this reason the others of my species were beginning to run in packs.

"You don't have to be like her," he said. He took a few steps away from me. "There are other creatures out there. Creatures who don't feed on humans. You don't have to feed on humans."

I tilted my head, trying to see farther into the trees. As the sun breached the horizon the priest seemed to fade farther into the trees, almost as if he was the one with a reason to be afraid of the sun.

"You don't know what I need." I made sure he could hear me. "I could tear you apart right now and drain your soul."

He stepped back into the light. A smile spread across his face and his arms were opened wide. "If you think you can." He gestured for me to come at him.

I crouched low and prepared to leap. A sudden crushing weight pinned me to the ground. Growling, I struggled against him, trying to force him off me. He hadn't moved except for a quick gesture with his hand. Another gesture and I was free.

"I could hold you here." He said. "I could call the Warrior and he would come and destroy you, like he did the others." He watched me with cold eyes. "I'm trying to save you, creature. Why won't you let me?"

"For someone who didn't know anything about us a few weeks ago you sure think you understand a lot now." I almost felt the need to shout the words at his retreating form.

"I've been studying." His voice was nearly nonexistent. "I didn't have much else to do since I left the church."

"Why did you leave?" I almost felt obligated to ask the question.

"I had another calling." His voice was muffled and seemed to be coming from a great distance. "You called to me, child."

I could no longer see him in the trees. The sun warmed my face and I could hear birds waking and calling to each other as they fluttered over the stream. Tiny fluttering creatures called as they scrounged through the brush searching for food. There was nothing in the woods to disturb them.

I felt drained. The rock was hard and was starting to get uncomfortable. Shrugging, I stood and adjusted my pack into place. It only took me seconds to climb to the top of the trail and make my way to the city. I needed to feed before I left Portland. I had no idea where I was headed and when I would find my next source of energy.

Chapter Thirteen

THE MOTORCYCLE THROBBED BETWEEN my legs as the miles flew by. I could feel the rhythm of the engine beating in my body, matching the rhythm of my heart. I still didn't know where I was headed, but I didn't care. All the weight of what I was leaving behind scattered in the wind. I left my past where it belonged, shredded and tattered by the force of the ride.

I had found the previous owner of the motorcycle passed out beside it outside of Club 205. I don't know which dancer cleaned out his wallet, but he didn't seem to be at all concerned about it. The drooling snores emanating from his slack lips showed a deliberate lack of concern. I dragged his great, hulking form into the alley and drained his energy. He gave it up easily. The keys had fallen to the ground beside the bike and his wife's leathers and helmet were tucked away in the saddle bags. She was only a little bigger than me so the clothes all fit. I had never ridden before, but I pulled the knowledge out of the head of my prey when I drained his energy.

The bike was a basic Harley, not very distinguishable from the thousands of other bikes on the road. I built up my energy around my body, creating a cloak around me and the bike. The humans may see me coming, but once I was outside of their field of perception they wouldn't take note of me. I would just be another faceless biker on a road trip.

I traveled south, like a migratory bird seeking the sun. I knew there were pockets of Were population scattered in major metropolitan areas. I wanted to avoid some of the large covens in the coastal cities. The families didn't like new blood in their territories feeding on their prey. I needed a city with a high transient population. A place where the missing stayed missing and random dead people barely created a blip on the radar. I turned the bike east and pushed over the mountains.

I couldn't explain exactly why I chose to travel this direction. There was a voice inside me telling me I needed to go. It wasn't safe where I was any more and I had to find new hunting grounds. The voice didn't tell me where to go, but I sensed a certain satisfaction when I finally settled on my destination.

The dry, desert air caressed my skin, bringing me to an entire new awareness. I felt light, unburdened, as the warm sun caressed my skin. The desert sparkled as the light reflected off the silica shards scattered in sand. Lizards and snakes sunned themselves in the roadway, unaware of the mechanisms of death bearing down on them. Some of the creatures managed to skitter out of the way before they were hit by the cars, but I passed more than one flattened, spread-out, form of the desert creatures pasted onto the freeway.

The lights of Vegas glowed for miles as I traveled throughout the night. It was two in the morning when I finally pulled off the freeway and into the heart of the city. I left the bike in a Wal-Mart parking lot a few blocks off the Strip. It was stolen property and even though I wasn't really worried about being harassed by the cops about it, I didn't need the albatross around my neck.

I needed to find a place to watch, to understand my new hunting ground. Vegas was a city in constant flux. There were covens here, but they were different from any of the covens I knew.

Agnes had taught me about covens. At least I think she taught me about them. Everything I knew about her was based on deception. I hoped my information about covens was accurate. Most covens fell into two categories based on their size. Large covens covered more territory and could hunt beyond their actual borders in relative safety. These larger covens controlled their members with strict codes of conduct. Smaller covens had less control of their members and their territories were, by necessity, much more defined. All covens would defend their territory with a vengeance, but the larger covens could easily carve out hunting grounds beyond their territories. They weren't very tolerant of strange Were anywhere near their hunting grounds.

My grandfather's coven was small, at least small compared to some of the covens in LA and New York. Portland had always been a Mecca for stray Were. My grandfather always tried to make contact with the wanderers and, if he liked them, would invite them to join his coven. It's how my father joined the coven. I wasn't too worried about my grandfather finding me in Vegas, his authority didn't extend much beyond the edges of the city of Portland. My only concern here was finding the defined territories of the covens of Vegas. I didn't want to wander into the hunting grounds of a powerful coven.

Most populated areas could only host one or, at the most, two covens. According to Agnes, Vegas had dozens. Every once in a while, coven wars would break out as one coven would try to expand their territory, but most of the time the covens operated within their defined territories, leaving the rest to their own devices. I needed to discover the boundaries of the territories so I could define my hunting grounds.

I started at Fremont Street. I could have started anywhere in the city, but I wanted to start in a central location and work my way out in an ever-increasing spiral. I would have the city figured out by the end of the week.

The energy spinning in the air was almost dizzying as I made my way through the crowds. I didn't dare draw any of it in because there is no faster way to gain the ire of a coven than to feed in their territory without consent. Even latent feeding, a skill I was more proficient at than most, could bring the wrath of coven leaders. I pulled my energy into myself and strolled down the sidewalk, avoiding even casual contact with other pedestrians.

I was able to identify other Were in the crowd. Were energy has a different quality than prey. It was almost as if the energy of the humans dimmed in contrast to the brightness of the Were. They watched me. I could feel the eyes of Were-creatures on me as I made my way down the street. None of them approached me, seeming to be satisfied with just observing my behavior and assessing any threats I may pose.

Heat reflected off the pavement, washing over me in waves. The smell of hot tar mingled with the scent of human sweat, flooding my nostrils and causing a thrill to creep up my spine. I reached out, gently probing the minds of those around me, wondering if I could lure one of the humans into a dark alley. I wasn't really hungry. I had overindulged before I left Portland and had fed again at a truck stop near the border outside of Medford. My head practically buzzed with energy.

I wanted to scale the walls of the buildings and run along the rooftops, but this wasn't like Portland. Everyone was out on the streets or hanging off balconies. Many of the rooftops were occupied by revelers taking advantage of the bright lights turning night into day. A rainbow of neon lights reflected off the buildings, changing the pale faces into twisted masques of humanity. My fingers curled into my palms as I fought the urge to grab at one and drain its energy.

A felt a thump against my backpack and immediately turned, raising my hands to protect my belongings. A woman stumbled against my sudden movement, straightened and staggered away. I watched her go, the green light of her energy flickered as she stumbled through the crowds and pushed her way through the door of a brightly lit building. The blue energy of a feeder followed close behind her. I knew the woman wouldn't survive the night.

I turned away from the feeder and his prey and continued down the street. The current of the crowd carried me forward, spinning me around obstacles and propelling me to an unknown destination. As we passed buildings entire groups would peel off and head towards the doors. I didn't even bother following. There was nothing in those buildings for me.

I could feel the energy of feeders oozing out of the very pores of the city. I wasn't sure if I would be able to identify the territories claimed by covens, but the longer I walked the more I could feel the vibration of the other feeders dominating the streets. The coven bonds were undeniable. The creatures' energies merged and bled into each other making their lights a prism of color. I'd never paid attention to coven Were before. I hadn't realized the bond between coven members went beyond just agreeing to work together. The energy of the Were I saw on the street melded together, interweaving and creating a bond of unbreakable fabric.

The crowd suddenly stopped, creating an impenetrable barrier across the breadth of the walkway. I tried to press through, but the mass of their bodies prevented me from moving forward. Human and Were pressed around me from all sides, forcing me to step back.

I caught a glimpse of three street performers dressed in brightly colored clothing leaping and pirouetting in the air. The red-garbed acrobat wore a full-face mask twisted in the macabre shape of a pointed-chin devil, complete with eight-inch bull's horns dyed red. He wore skin-tight, knee-length pants and nothing else, although his body was covered all over with brightly colored body paints of red and yellow flames. It looked like the flames of Hell had reached out and engulfed him in fiery glory. The other two performers were dressed just like him sans the mask, but their bodies were panted in pastel blues and yellows. The colors perfectly matched the colors of their souls.

The performance lasted just a few moments and at the end the three filtered through the crowd gathering the coins and the green slips of paper held out by the crowd. They gathered a little more than money. With each touch of the hand or casual brush against a body the three Were drained a little bit of energy from the members of the milling crowd. The crowd thinned out and I prepared to move forward again, but a hand reached out and wrapped around my arm. The grip was strong, but not strong enough. I could have easily broken the hold, but I didn't feel any threat from my captor and trying to fight him might draw unwanted attention from others.

Gentle pressure on my arm led me to a tiny alley between two massive buildings. I could feel the presence of the other Were as we stepped deeper into the shadows. I stopped before they had the chance to back me into a corner, planting my feet and not moving forward was enough to let them know they couldn't completely control me. We were deep enough in the alley to be hidden from casual observers, but I could still hear the sounds of revelers and catch an occasional glimpse of a body walking by.

I couldn't make out the face of my captor. He was completely hidden in shadow. Normally this wouldn't be a problem for me, but he was also pulling in his energy and hiding his aura from me. The Were holding me captive was powerful, almost as powerful as Agnes. I focused on the bright light at the center of his aura. There were many threads flowing through the core of his being. Brightly colored strings of light flowed into his soul and were bound tightly together in a great mass. I felt myself drawn to him. There was a compulsion to reach in and touch the light. I could feel the seductive threads calling to me. Lifting my foot, I nearly took a step forward. A sharp command from inside my head stayed my action. This was not where I needed to be. There was something better out there for me. I shook off the compulsion and pulled my energy into my core.

Sudden movement drew my attention to the mouth of the alley. The street performers had joined me and my companion in the alley. I turned to face them, stepping to the center of the space to allow for the greatest range of motion in case I had to move quickly.

Chapter Fourteen

THEY TRIED TO CIRCLE around me, coming at me on all sides. The light of their energy flowed around me, weaving a brightly woven cage, entrapping my own energy and binding me. I pulled my energy into my core and built a wall between us. I could push my energy out, collapsing their cage and make my escape, but they would just chase me down or another coven would sense me and move in for the capture, or the kill. If I was going to hedge my bets and see what I was facing I might as well start here. I glanced at the creature in the devil costume and allowed my lips to curl up in a sneer. He wasn't the leader of the coven, but his energy was the strongest in the group. I made sure I was looking at the leader, but I directed my comments to the devil.

"Really, guys," I said. "A dark alley in Vegas, can we get any more cliché?"

The leader stepped out of the shadows and motioned for the others to step back. He was a handsome, wide-eyed boy in simple tee-shirt and jeans.

"Well, we could always move this meeting to my deep, dark basement lair," he said. I could hear the laughter in his voice. "You're new here." It was a statement, not a question. "We want to make sure you understand the rules before you decide to go hunting."

"Do you run the town?" I knew the answer to my question before I asked, but I needed to look like I was playing by the rules.

"This part of it I do." His statement was obviously a lie. He was building up a sense of false bravado, trying to make himself seem important.

"What do I need to know?" I tried to keep the sneer out of my voice. I don't think I succeeded.

"You're in my coven's territory." His tone revealed he hadn't caught the sarcasm in my voice. "We control Freemont Street all the way down to the top of the Vegas Strip. Don't even bother going to the Strip. Welhiem's coven controls it right now, but there's another battle brewing over that territory. The territory around the Strip and some of the hot-bed casinos are always being disputed. If you're an unaffiliated Were it's best to just avoid the territories. The last thing you want to do is get caught in the crossfire of a coven war."

"Is there anywhere in this town where I can hunt?" I asked.

"A few, but the pickings are slim." He smiled. I'm sure his smile would be considered charming if he tried it on anyone else besides me. "Of course, you could become affiliated. You could avoid all sorts of problems if you became affiliated."

There it was, the threat. The way he said the words, I knew the problems I would need to avoid would mostly come from him.

He was watching me expectantly. I wasn't quite sure what he was expecting. Obviously, he was offering me a place in his coven. It isn't uncommon for Were to form immediate bonds with outsiders. We can read each other's energy and automatically know if an intruder intends to challenge the authority of a coven. This Were wanted to control the Strip. He read my energy and could see I didn't intend to encroach on his territory.

His control of the territory must be tenuous to offer me a place in the coven so quickly. He needed numbers on his side if it came down to a battle. I wasn't interested in getting involved in turf wars between covens. I just wanted to know where I could find prey.

I shifted from one foot to the other, centering myself against attack. Having to fight my way out of the alley was becoming a real possibility. I thought about dropping my pack, but I didn't want to leave it behind. I wasn't sure if I would have time to pick it up once I finished with these fools.

I had never actually fought another Were before. The Were in Portland tended to live and let live. I knew how to fight, though. The memories and knowledge of the souls I had feasted on blazed through my mind as I analyzed the best way to fight these boys. I had taken on skilled soldiers, martial arts masters, bar fighters and street fighters and had beaten them all. These boys, and boys they were, were close to my age. Coming to a new town and starting a fight with the locals probably wasn't the best idea. I forced the fighting instinct down somewhere into my toes and smiled at the leader.

"Well, I just barely made it into town." I kept my voice light, quite an accomplishment for me. I was proud of myself. "I don't even know how long I'm going to be staying. Joining a coven might make it awkward when I decide to move on."

"If you chose not to join a coven you better move on fast." He took a step closer to me, his lips curling into a sneer.

"Vague threats and veiled innuendos don't really frighten me." I maintained my position. Backing up now would mean I was running away from him.

The other Were stepped closer, blocking the exit of the alley and slowly closing in on me with web-like precision. Their energy cage tightened, closing off any possible gaps. I smiled and slowly curled my hands into fists. The alley was narrow, blocked off at the end behind me by two overflowing dumpsters. The members of the coven were closing in on me, trying to push me into the wall. There were advantages to putting my back to the wall. I would only have to defend myself from three sides, not four, but I would also be cornered and not have an avenue of escape. I stood my ground.

I ducked under the leader's arms when he reached for me and jabbed him in the rib cage. As I did, I released the energy building in my core. His bones cracked under my fist and I could feel his hot breath on the back of my neck as he exhaled forcefully. It wasn't a fatal blow, but the injury was not an easy one from which to recover. As he bent over I brought my knee to his face and his nose and cheek bone collapsed. Blood spilled out of his broken nose and dripped onto my pant leg. He collapsed, wrapping one arm around his ribcage and bringing the other to his face to try to staunch the flow of dark, red fluid.

The smell of blood filled my nostrils and my throat tightened with the memory of the blood my mother drank before I was born. I shook off the sensation and turned my attention to the three other members of the coven, I positioned myself so I could see all my attackers at once. The alley was narrow and they couldn't spread out to come at me from multiple angles. The coven leader sat huddled against the far wall. He wasn't going to come back into the fight any time soon.

I had seen enough of the street performance to know the three trying to box me in were agile and quick, but I had no idea which one was the strongest. The smell of sweat was in the air. They may have been Were, but they weren't very strong. I doubted they even had the ability to change shape. Latent feeders rarely had the ability to do more than draw residual energy off prey. The massive amounts of energy required for healing and shape change was astronomical. I didn't need to kill, I just needed to maim. It would be enough of a warning to keep them away from me for a while.

The two smaller Were attacked at the same time. Devil-face was holding back. I could see his strategy as clearly as if I thought of it myself. Let the others weaken me and he would come in for the kill later, when he thought I couldn't take any more. His arrogance oozed off his body like a film of slime on a pond.

As the two Were rushed towards me I leapt into the air, flipped backwards and landed on top of the dumpster. My attackers weren't quite as quick as I was and they were left standing opposite each other staring at the place I where I was just standing. I contemplated leaping to the balcony of the building and racing across the rooftop before the others could figure out what happened, but I didn't want to leave them in a condition to follow me out of the alley.

Before the others could figure out where I disappeared to, I jumped off the dumpster, flipping through the air and landed behind them. I kneecapped one of them and then, with a spinning roundhouse, kicked the other one on the head. I felt the crunch of his skull under the ball of my foot. Both of them collapsed to the ground. I punched the kneecapped victim in the throat, quieting his groans of pain. The last thing I needed was a curious tourist who didn't know any better investigating strange noises coming from the alley.

Three down, one to go. I turned to devil-face, preparing to take him down like I did the others. He still hadn't moved any closer to me. I knew he was studying me. I could feel the energy exuding off his body as he contemplated his next actions. His eyes flashed through the mask, taking in the forms of the other Were, each in a different state of consciousness. I sent a probing thought out, trying to catch the images in his mind. I realized he wasn't focusing on me. All his energy was focused on the twitching forms of my opponents.

I slowly moved away from the huddled bodies at my feet. The Devil's eyes didn't move to follow me as I edged towards the alley opening. I was a few feet from the injured Were when he made his move. He was fast, almost as fast as me. In one move he flew to the leader of the pack and grabbed him by the front of his shirt. He peeled the mask from his face and brought his mouth down on the bloody lips of his prey. I caught a glimpse of his face as he moved towards his victim. His skin was brown with patchy blotches of white. Most startling was his eyes. Ice blue eyes rimmed with a thick black ring watched me as he drew the energy from the coven leader.

My entire body shuddered at the image of the creature feasting on another Were. His ribcage expanded and contracted and his spine hunched as he drew the energy from his victim's body. I could feel when he broke through the protective barrier every

Were possesses to keep other soul-eaters from feasting on their energy. His actions became more frantic as his prey struggled beneath him. I could see his shoulder blades tense as they cut a sharp angle in the red body paint.

The body of his victim seemed to shrink as the devil drained him. The lights of their energy bounced off each other, creating a laser show within the narrow space their bodies were occupying. Dark red against bright blue. It was beautiful. Startling, but beautiful. The light faded and the devil dropped the shriveled body of the coven leader to the ground. His body collapsed in on itself, slowly crumbling to dust.

The devil turned to the other two victims. His mouth was covered in blood from the coven leader and, as he turned, his tongue slowly dragged across his lips. His smile told me he was savoring the sweet, tangy salt of the warm blood. He glanced at me and then turned to the other two shattered bodies on the ground. I saw his intent in his eyes. He was closer to them than I was, but I was faster. I covered the distance before he could and positioned myself between him and the bodies on the ground.

Chapter Fifteen

I STOOD IN FRONT of the broken bodies of my opponents, my feet spread wide and my arms held in my favorite fighting stance. The smile dropped off his face as his lips curled away from his teeth and a growl rumbled from the back of his throat.

"You don't need both of them." His tongue darted out to swipe at more of the blood. "You'll take one and I'll take the other."

I didn't move from my position.

"Listen," his voice oozed confidence. "I can feel your strength. I think every coven in the city felt you when you rolled into town. You're young, though. Maybe too young. You have a lot to learn. If you team up with me I will teach you what you need to know. Together we can rule this town."

He was powerful. More powerful than I first realized. I could feel his energy rolling off his body in waves. He reached into my mind, probing and stabbing at my thoughts, trying to force me to open myself to him. It took every ounce of skill I had learned from Agnes to keep myself closed from his assault. Finally, he pulled back, closing himself from me.

"You may leave now." His eyes turned back to the others. "No one will know what you did here, I'll make sure of that."

I didn't move from my position in front of the two Were. "I'm not going to let you take the life of these two creatures. They're helpless and you don't need to feed any more. You are full and to feed on them would just be gluttony."

The devil laughed. He took a step towards me to force me back. I didn't move.

"Are you telling me that you, a soul-eater, a harbinger of death, you actually have a conscious?" He smiled and took another step forward. "These two are weak. Even their leader was weak. I joined them because I knew they would eventually try to take on an opponent stronger than them. It's easy to feast on the energy of soul-eaters if you weaken them first. I could teach you how, if you joined me."

His tongue darted out again, taking another swipe at the blood on his chin. I could feel his satisfaction at the taste. He savored the taste of blood as much as he did the taste of energy.

"I don't want to learn anything from you." I didn't even bother to disguise the disgust in my voice. "Leave now. You're not going to feed on these two."

He took another step and I readied my stance. He grinned as his tongue darted in and out of his mouth, lizard-like in its efficiency.

"Perhaps I will taste your soul, then."

As he lunged toward me I ducked and rolled to the side, taking a swipe at his ribs with a clawed hand. He landed too close to the others for my comfort. I picked up a broken chunk of cement, about the size of my fist, and pitched it as hard as I could against his back. It landed with a solid thunk. A welt appeared on his back emphasized by a trickle of blood. His face was curled into an angry sneer when he turned back to look at me.

"Why do you insist on protecting them?"

I could see the scratches on his rib cage. They were still streaked with the red of his blood, but the injury had sealed and the bruising around his ribs was already starting to fade. His healing power was obviously much stronger than his companions.

He was still too close to the others for my comfort. I could see the two forms twitch and start to struggle to their feet. Their wounds were healing, but I could still see them struggling to get their bearings. Pushing my energy towards them I sent the command for them to run. The devil staggered with the force of my thoughts. He stared at me, rage filled his eyes and his lips peeled back from his teeth in a sneer.

"Bitch!" Spittle flew from his mouth with the force of the ejaculated word. "You are dead. I hope you know that."

His words burned into my chest, igniting anger to flare through my head. Crouching, I prepared to leap at him. His shoulders shifted and he ran towards me. I bounced on the balls of my feet and slashed out at his eyes, spinning away before he could ensnare me in his grasp.

He hissed as he wiped blood from his face and eyes. Before he could orient himself to my location I jumped on his back and wrapped my arms around his throat. Arching his back, he tried to buck me off like a mad bull at a rodeo. I wrapped my legs around his torso and raked a clawed hand across his face.

His rib cage expanded as he drew in his breath. Tightening my legs, I cut off his air supply and jammed the knuckle of my thumb into the soft tissue under his jaw. He dropped to the ground and hunched over, gagging and gasping for breath. I rolled to my feet and prepared to spring at him again. A shadow blocked the light filtering from the street and we both turned to face the new encroacher on our battle.

The two Were I had been protecting took the opportunity provided by the distraction to scramble out of the alley. I studied the new creature slowly creeping into the darkness of our battle ground. His soul was dark and yet it seemed to glow brighter than any Were I had ever seen before. He didn't have any markings connecting him to my opponent, but if he was here to fight it didn't really matter. He was just as dangerous as the monster standing at my right. I glanced at the devil. He seemed shriveled and dark and his eyes lost their intense burn as he watched the shadowy figure inch towards us.

"Welhiem." The name was a whisper, but his voice crackled with fear.

The devil flipped backwards and flew out of the alley. I didn't watch him go. I was more interested in the man approaching from the entrance.

A flash of light brightened the darkness for a moment, giving me a glimpse of his features. His dark hair was sprinkled with grey and stood out from his head in flyaway spikes. His face was narrow with high cheek bones and a large, sharp pointed nose. Dark eyes peered out from red-rimmed sockets in his pale-white face. Thinned lips peeled away from gleaming white teeth and I realized he was smiling at me.

"Well, it looks like you've met the welcoming committee." His voice carried an undertone of laughter and I couldn't help but be drawn to the charismatic energy flowing from his form.

I glanced around the alley. There wasn't any evidence of our epic battle. Even the dusty remains of the dead Were had been picked up by the wind and had mingled with the other dust and debris in the alley. The man standing in front of me gave a slight bow and extended his arm towards the opening of the alley.

"Perhaps we should continue this somewhere a little less public?" His voice was smooth and soothing. "These humans rarely notice things they don't understand, or at least they prefer not to notice them, but there's always the off chance one of them has the ability to see through the veil."

A wave of warmth flooded over me and the voice in my head whispered for me to trust him. His energy washed over me, soothing me in his bright warmth. He was my safe harbor. I followed him into the brightness of the street. He led me through the crowd, guiding me with subtle signals to turn right or left. My speed was unchecked by the crowds and uninhibited by the pack on my back. The crowds were standing shoulder to shoulder, yet when we moved we didn't bump into any bodies or brush against elbows.

We stayed in the crowds, moving even deeper into the city. It only took a few minutes to walk the length of the Strip, but we didn't leave the lights behind. The sky glowed with the brightness of the neon lights reflecting off the glass fronts of buildings. It seemed we had walked for miles, passing through neighborhoods bereft of the bright lights of casinos. The houses looked like any you would find in the suburbs of Portland. If it wasn't for the jarring lights of casinos in random locations I could almost believe I was home.

We walked for miles to the outskirts of the city and beyond. He led me to a brightly lit house with a sprawling wide, green lawn. I hadn't seen much green in this city, but these lawns didn't have the dark green of the grass I was used to in Portland. The light green, sage coloring and sharp, wide leaves thrust out at different angles from the sandy soil, much like the hair growing in sharp relief from my scalp. We had walked away from the city into an area close to the mountains. It hadn't taken much time at all to walk the distance, but we were moving at such a fast pace it had taken some of my energy reserve. I wondered how long it would have taken for me to walk from Portland to Vegas at the pace we had set. Probably not much more than it would have taken me to ride, but I would have had to feed more frequently.

The door opened before we even made it up the three steps to the wide front porch. A small, dumpy looking woman was holding the door open for us and she smiled as we walked across the threshold.

"Welcome back Master Welhiem," she said. "It looks like you brought us another stray."

The woman's face had an ageless quality to it. She could have been fifty or five-hundred. I narrowed my eyes and tried to study her, but she knew what I was doing and her smile widened. I was surprised to see the friendly sparkle in her eyes. A soft violet glow manifested over her body. She wasn't a Were, but she had the markings of power about her energy.

"Good evening, Darlene. Our new friend needs something to eat." The man shrugged out of his coat and draped it across a hook on a coat rack standing in the hall. "I think we have some fresh fruit and maybe a peanut butter sandwich. Just something to hold her over until dinner."

Darlene closed the door and scurried down the hall. As she disappeared around the corner I turned back to the man who had led me to this house. He was staring at me, a smile playing at the corners of his mouth. I ducked my head, hoping he would lose interest and stop staring me.

"Why don't you come and meet the rest of the family." He gestured for me to follow him down the hall.

I followed him into a brightly lit room crowded with couches and overstuffed lounge chairs. Everything was white: carpet, couches, even the lampshades resting on end tables scattered around the room were white. Before I stepped on to the white carpeting I inspect my shoes, looking for any dirt particles. I'm usually clean, but the carpet was so pristine I really didn't want to track any dirt into the room.

Three people were sitting on the scattered furniture. They were laughing and talking over the top of each other so quickly I couldn't understand their words. The words and laughter stopped as I stepped into the room. Three pairs of eyes bore into me. I could feel them studying me and judging my strength.

"Children, welcome our new friend," Welhiem said.

My brain was still trying to wrap around the word friend as the three Were stood and approached me. They surrounded me in a tight circle, embracing me and rubbing my shoulders. I was engulfed in warmth and could feel strength flowing through my body. It was almost as if they were feeding me energy. The creatures were murmuring words of welcome as they led me to the couch and encouraged me to sit.

Within a few minutes Darlene delivered a tray of food and everyone was eating and talking as if I had been in the home for a hundred years. I still hadn't said a word, but I could feel my energy reaching out to the others, weaving in with their brightly hued souls and creating a bond I knew would never be severed. For the first time in my life I felt as if I was home.

Chapter Sixteen

IT DIDN'T TAKE ME long to adapt to my new family. The man who brought me to the house introduced himself as Bartholomew Welhiem. Darlene was the only one who called him Master Welhiem. The other three occupants of the house called him father. I didn't call him anything. This was all just too new for me.

After I had eaten, Darlene showed me to a bedroom complete with bed and a closet full of clothes. She handed me a towel and directed me to a bathroom. I was hesitant to drop my pack and strip out of my clothes, but I hadn't taken a shower in a few days and my clothes were covered with road dust. At least I didn't stink, a benefit of not having sweat glands. The lure of a hot shower was too much for me and once she left me alone I stripped out of my clothes and took advantage of the marble sheathed enclosure.

I pulled on my last pair of clean pants and shirt and stuffed my dirty clothes back in my bag. The cans rattled around in the bottom of the pack. I hadn't eaten very much of the food I had with me, relying on the energy I had feasted on during my journey to keep me going.

Darlene was waiting for me when I left the bathroom. She shook her head but was smiling as she looked me up and down.

"You can leave your belongings in your room," she said as she led me back down the hall. "There's a washer and dryer in the basement if you want to wash your clothes. Dinner's on the table and the rest of the family is looking forward to getting to know you better."

My first meal with this new coven was awkward. Or, at least it was on my part. Welhiem sat at the head of the table directing food service and leading conversation. The others dished out food and information in equal measure. Welhiem's coven was much larger than the occupants of his home. I could see the energy of countless Were interwoven in the fabric of his energy. The family in the home consisted of two females and a male Were he called his children and Darlene. I could tell by their energy signature the only ones who were genetically related were the two Were females, but the auras of all of them had the markings of a coven bond. A bond which was sometimes stronger than any familial ties found in human society.

The food Darlene served for dinner was beautiful and full of flavor. A roasted chicken dominated the table, but there were also potatoes and bread, salad and roasted vegetables. I ate everything except the chicken. The others watched me out of the corner of their eyes as I hunched over my plate and shoveled the food in with my fork. I chewed each mouthful just enough to safely swallow before taking another bite. Eating too slow in the foster homes or the asylums was a way to get your food stolen from your plate. No one said anything, but I could feel them judging me. I was only about halfway through my meal, but I pushed my plate away and leaned back in my seat.

The dining room entrance was only a few paces away. I measured the distance with my eyes, calculating how long it would take to make it out the door, back to the bedroom to grab my belongings and jump out of the window to make a get-away. Welhiem caught my eye and gave me a gentle smile. A feeling of warmth and security filled my body and I allowed myself to relax. At least he wasn't judging me. I pulled my plate back towards me and finished my meal, slowing down and savoring each bite.

"So, tell us about yourself, child." Welhiem's voice was soothing, but I could feel the compulsion to talk being pulled out of me. "Starting with your name and why you decided to leave the O'Connell coven to strike out on your own."

I swallowed my last bite of food before I answered. I at least knew enough about manners to not talk with my mouth full. "My name's Maria Christine. Most people call me Mary." By most people I meant Agnes and Sophia. I never really talked to anyone else. "I'm not an O'Connell. At least I wasn't raised one. I've never been part of a Coven so it wasn't that big of a deal to leave and come here."

"How did you learn to become such a powerful soul-eater if you weren't raised in a coven?" The question came from the boy sitting directly across from me.

"Manners, Stephen." Welhiem's voice was gentle, but the reprimand was clear. "We must first introduce ourselves and build trust with our new friend before asking too many personal questions."

Stephen lowered his eyes to his plate and started pushing his food around with his fork. "Yes, father. I'm sorry. I didn't mean to be rude."

"It's okay, son." Welhiem turned his attention back to me. "Stephen is the newest member of our coven. He's only been with us a few months and sometimes it's hard for him to remember we are a civilized family. Helena and her daughter Cassandra have been with me for many years. You may not believe this, but they are older than Darlene. She joined our family nearly three hundred and fifty years ago. Her story is quite dramatic, but it is her story to tell, if she chooses to share. It's hard overcoming our pasts, especially when the past involves running with some of the feral covens."

My mind flashed back to the devil and the coven from the alley. There was a wild quality about them I recognized from some of the more loosely organized covens in Portland.

I had never thought about how Were viewed themselves as part of the human society. In my mind we were the feeder and they were the prey. I needed to consume their energy to survive. If I didn't my body would turn in on itself and slowly consume me from the inside out. I would never be able to take in enough food to keep my body nourished and healthy. The only reason I kept up any human façade at all was so I could move among them with ease and seek out my victims. I know many Were aren't as selective as I was when it came time to feed, but not all Were can completely drain an entire human at one sitting like I can. It usually takes multiple feedings or multiple Were to completely drain a human.

Welhiem passed the platter holding the whole roasted chicken towards me, gesturing to the white flesh cut away from the bones.

"Would you like some chicken?" He pushed some breast meat towards my plate with his fork. I guarded my plate with my hand before he could transfer the piece.

"I'm sorry," I whispered, unsure of how the others would react to my refusal of the food. "I don't eat meat."

Welhiem pulled the platter back, quickly placing it as far away from me as he could reach. "I'm sorry, I should have realized you were a vegan. I usually don't make such a social faux pas."

I shook my head, deciding an explanation was necessary. "I'm not a vegan. I don't even think I can be classified as a vegetarian. I just can't stand the taste of blood-filled flesh. Eggs and dairy products don't bother me. It's just the blood tainting the flesh of the beasts I can't stand."

The others at the table were staring, judging me with their eyes. I stiffened in my seat, ready for the challenge. One by one they each lowered their eyes to their plates. I glanced at Welhiem. He smiled and handed me a bowl holding soft, white dinner rolls.

"Well, don't be afraid to eat anything in this house." He gestured for the others to pass food around the table. "We always have plenty. It won't take you long to fit in here."

I took the roll and started tearing it apart with my fingers. It was buttery and soft, fresher than any of the rolls I had at the soup kitchens. The others stopped watching me and focused on their own plates.

"I hope you will learn to trust us, child." Welhiem's voice was gentle and soothing. "This will be your home as long as you wish to stay. I have sensed your power, as I am sure you have sensed mine. You have a discerning spirit about you, otherwise you wouldn't have been so willing to fight Sebastian in the alley or follow me home when I invited you."

The others looked up when they heard Sebastian's name mentioned. Their eyes took on a new appreciation as they studied me. Welhiem's smile eased the tension as he passed me the platter of fresh, sliced fruit.

"Sebastian was one of us once." I studied the tight faces of the other Were as Welhiem told the story. "I found the others as I found you. As I have found many others over the centuries. Most of my children stay with me for a while and then, when they grow up, move off on their own. Some of them have succumbed to the ravages of age or were killed by Warriors. Sebastian made his own path a few years ago."

I finished the roll and reached for my glass of water. My fingers slid against the glass from the buttery leftovers of the bread. I let go of the glass before it could drop and wiped my fingers on my pants without even thinking about it. It didn't take much to wipe off the mess since there wasn't anything for the butter to bond with on my skin. The fabric absorbed the oily substance easily. Welhiem lifted his linen napkin to his lips, gently wiping at nonexistent crumbs. I glanced at the folded square of cloth sitting next to my plate, untouched and sparkling white. I had never seen a cloth napkin before, but now I realized I was expected to use this pristine piece of cloth to clean my dirty fingers. I picked up the cloth and placed it across my lap. Welhiem smiled and returned to the conversation.

"You have amazing fighting instincts, child." Welhiem said. "I've never seen anyone take on four Were and survive, let alone hold their own. With a little bit of training you could be a real force to be reckoned with."

Welhiem's smile was open and genuine. I could feel the warmth radiating off his body as his energy reached out to mine. It was the first time in my existence I knew a Were wanted to help me without wanting anything in return.

I studied the faces of the others at the table. Everyone had finished eating and were just sitting at the table watching the interaction between me and Welhiem. For the first time I really took notice of the others at the table. Stephen had a very serious expression on his face as he studied me. His blue eyes weren't exactly hostile, more guarded than anything. His pale skin seemed almost translucent and his face was all angles and cheekbones. I realized the cut of his jaw was very similar to mine. Long blond hair was clubbed back but draped over his neck to about halfway down his shoulders. He was very appealing and I could imagine many humans were drawn to his natural magnetism.

Helena and Cassandra were nearly mirror images of each other. If Welhiem hadn't mentioned they were mother and daughter I would have assumed they were twins. They were both small and dark with long brown hair and golden-brown eyes. Pretty. It's the only word I could think of when I looked at them. They weren't beautiful. Their bodies were too slim and wiry and their faces too angular to be considered beautiful, but I knew they were prettier than I could ever be.

This was my new family. I could already feel the bonds of the Coven tying us together. There was a warmth building in the center of my chest and spreading through my entire body. In just the few hours I had been there I was already feeling like I was home.

Darlene placed a platter pilled high with roasted vegetables and bread next to my plate. I looked for Welhiem's nod of approval before reaching for the serving spoons. Carefully avoiding touching the food with my fingers, I took a serving of vegetables and more bread. Warmth flooded over me Welhiem graced me with a gentle smile. Tomorrow I would learn more about the hunt, but today I was warm and fed.

Chapter Seventeen

THE MEAL HAD FILLED my body, but my energy was low. I knew I needed to hunt, but I needed to know where I could go to find ready prey. I wasn't sure how to broach the subject with my new coven leader as we all joined in the chore of clearing the table and doing the dishes. Once the dishwasher was loaded and most of the leftovers were put away in the huge stainless-steel fridge, Darlene shooed us out of the kitchen.

We all gathered in the living room. The vast open space was filled with strategically placed furniture arranged in tight circles so small groups could gather and talk facing each other. It was a comfortable place. A place for closeness and sharing. Welhiem led us to a sitting area with overstuffed white chairs and a loveseat. The furniture looked so clean I was afraid to sit on it because of the stains on my pants. He insisted I sit, so I gingerly lowered myself into a chair, sitting only on the very edge.

Light filtered in through the cut glass windows, creating a prism of color dancing through the room. I wondered how much time had passed since I entered the house. It could have only been a few hours at most. Time wasn't important to me. Humans put great store in the concept of time, allowing it to dictate when they ate, when they slept, when they socialized, when they mated. My life was dictated by the needs of my body. I ate when I was hungry, hunted when I needed energy, rested when my body needed rest and I never mated.

I had only entered menses twice in my life, but I was still young and the urge to mate hadn't been overpowering as much as Agnes told me it could be. I still had a few years before the urge would be strong enough to override every instinct and drive me to seek a mate. I would just have to make sure I was far away from any human or Were when it happened. There was no parental instinct anywhere in my being. I had no desire to ever have a child of my own.

The others were all staring at me. Cassandra and Helena were sitting on the loveseat directly across from me. Stephen and Welhiem sat in chairs on either side of me. The air vibrated with repressed energy. Helena took Cassandra's hand and reached for Stephen's. On the other side, Cassandra reached for Welhiem and grasped his outstretched hand. Welhiem and Stephen reached towards me. I stared at their hands, not comprehending what they wanted at first. Slowly, I reached out and took hold of Welhiem's outstretched hand. With a little more hesitancy, I spread my fingers towards Stephen. His hand was soft and warm as it engulfed mine. A sudden jolt of energy buzzed through me, causing the hair on my head to nearly stand on end.

My body filled with the energy of the others, satiating my desire to feed. I felt the weight of their past filling my mind with their personal history. Centuries of experiences rushed through me, tying my soul with theirs. Images flooded my mind, twisting and building like a fire, burning away my own past and binding me to them.

I pulled back my hands and sat in silence. Images flashed through my mind. Glimpses of a past that did not belong to me. I could feel my brain shifting through the information and storing it away to be processed later. There were no words. There wasn't a need for words. I knew them and they knew me.

Welhiem smiled at me and stretched out his hand to lift me from my seat.

"Let me show you around your new home, Maria." He led me from the room. The others followed close behind.

"We'll go hunting tonight," he said as he led me to the rear of the house. "You'll learn how to hunt in a coven and share your energy. When you feed you fill yourself so full of energy you can't process it fast enough. That's why you have seizures. By the time I finish teaching you what you need to know you'll be able to feed without fearing the seizures." I didn't ask him how he knew about the seizures. He had touched me at the core of my soul. I had no secrets from him.

He led me down the stairs to a wide, open room with wood floors and cement walls all covered with padded mats. The walls were lined floor to ceiling with bright, shining weapons. Daggers and swords, spears, knives, all types of weaponry created for close combat. I scanned the walls, looking for any weapon designed to separate fighting combatants, a gun, bow and arrows, anything. There was nothing there. Everything in the room was designed to bring combatants as close to each other as possible.

I reached for a sword and lifted it from the wall. Feeling the weight, I hefted it over my shoulder and prepared to swing it forward. Welhiem moved in front of me, staying my hand.

"Don't hold it like a baseball bat." He adjusted my hands so the blade was positioned vertical in front of my body. "Allow the blade to become an extension of your arm."

The weight of the blade pulled at my wrists and I couldn't quite get the balance of it. Welhiem plucked it from my grasp and replaced it on the wall.

"There will be time enough to learn this craft." He said. "Come, let me show you what else we have."

He opened a door and I stepped out into the heat of the desert. Huge rock walls and towering structures littered the landscape. Even as I studied the structures I put together what they were designed for. This was the perfect training grounds.

I rushed forward and quickly climbed to the top of one of the rock towers. This was my element. I stood on top of the tower and looked down at the others. Welhiem's teeth flashed white in the sunlight as he grinned up at me.

"Such raw skill," he said. "You will be a glorious creature when I finish with you."

I smiled down at him. "Why do I need training? I already know how to feed."

"Did you know how to defeat Agnes when she tried to steal your body? What about Sebastian?" He asked. "You can hold your own in a fight, yes. But, I can teach you how to fight and defeat other Were."

I studied the faces of the Were staring up at me. Stephen's face was set in a grim, thoughtful expression. He seemed angry, but I knew he wasn't angry at me. Cassandra's mouth was open in a wide smile, looking like she was on the verge of laughter. I couldn't help myself. Pulling myself up to the tip of my toes, I did my best to mimic a ballerina en pointe. My perch was precarious, but I wasn't afraid of falling. I was too well balanced to fall.

"Why would I target Were?" I asked. "There is plenty of human fodder out there."

"We don't target Were." Welhiem motioned for me to come down off my perch and join him. I sprang from the top of the rock and flipped, landing on the balls of my feet directly in front of Cassandra. She smiled and grabbed my hand, walking with me as Welhiem continued his explanation.

"We feed on human souls, just like you," he explained. "You seek out humans who contribute little to this world. Those who are in pain or cause pain to others. So do we, for the most part. But other Were aren't as discriminating as we are when they feed. Or, like Sebastian, they encroach on our territory and need to be put in their place."

I could see Stephen's face tighten at the mention of Sebastian's name. Cassandra reached out and linked her arm with his, leading us behind Welhiem as he continued through the yard. We covered the few acres in only a few minutes.

"The energy we get from Were is different than human energy. It's more substantial. Even now you are feeling the effects of the energy your brother and sisters have given you." I looked at the others as we walked behind Welhiem. I could feel the warmth of Cassandra's energy against my hand. "There are consequences to feeding on Were though. It's addictive and can sometimes drive a creature to the edges of insanity."

"That's what happened to Sebastian." Cassandra's voice was clear and sweet. She spoke so quietly I almost had to lean in to hear her. "He developed a taste for Were souls. He's killed more

Were in the past five years than I have in my entire lifetime."

Welhiem led us back into the practice room. He led me to the center of the room and had me stand with my arms held out like wings. He walked around me in circles, pushing against my arms, rocking me back and forth, feeling my muscles on my arms, legs and stomach. Smiling, he ran his fingers through my short, spiky hair and patted my cheek.

"You're older than you look, but not by much." He gestured for me to relax and sit on a pile of exercise mats. "You're also stronger than you look. How fast can you run?"

I shrugged and thought for a moment. "I've never really run in my human form. I'm fast, but mostly I jump from building to building. Running in city streets tends to draw unwanted attention."

"Well," he said. "We will teach you how to work and not draw attention to yourself. You already have skills far greater than Were of your age. Agnes taught you well. It's too bad she abused you so horribly."

I didn't think Agnes really abused me. She always made sure I had food and she taught me how to protect my energy from Hunters and Warriors. It wasn't until she tried to take possession of my body that I really had any reason to fear her. The painful memory caused me to shudder and I wrapped my arms around my torso.

"How do you know Agnes?" I asked.

"There aren't many Were as ancient as Agnes and me in this world." Welhiem explained. "We've crossed paths a few times in our centuries of existence. I'll tell you all about it, when the time comes."

The others moved to different areas of the room. Stripping off their jackets, they revealed tight-fitting tank tops and snug stretch pants. All three had tight, rippling muscles denoting their strength. They stretched and contorted their bodies, demonstrating their power. My own body was thin and wiry compared to theirs.

"Darlene probably has your wardrobe figured out by now." Welhiem gestured for me to follow him back into the main house. "I think you'll find it easier to hunt and train in the clothes she picked out for you. I hope you don't mind giving up your old clothes. She also got rid of the cans of food you had packed away. As long as you're living with us you will be provided for body and soul."

Welhiem led me back up the stairs to the bedrooms. "Don't be afraid to explore the house," he said. "There is no space off-limits. We have no secrets here."

He opened the door to my room and stood aside. The bed stared at me from across the room. For a moment I wished I did sleep. The white cotton sheets and tan bedspread covering the deep mattress looked inviting.

"Thank you for the offer of the room," I said. "But, I don't sleep. I won't make much use of the bed."

Welhiem smiled and stepped into the room. "You wouldn't be the first child I had who didn't sleep," he said. "You're nearly a full-blooded Were so I'm not surprised. The rest of us don't sleep long hours either. I'm sure you'll find something to do to occupy your time. The others all have. Now, there are things to do other than sleep in this room. We have a library, so you can read. You can listen to music. This is your room, do whatever you need to do to make it yours."

I looked around the space he was designating a mine. The entire room was bigger than my apartment in Portland. As I stepped inside I realized this was only part of the life he was offering me. I still hadn't seen the rest of the house.

Chapter Eighteen

DARLENE HAD CLEANED OUT the closet of any extra clothing, leaving me with nothing but dark, snug-fitting tanks, tee shirts and pants. The wardrobe was simple, but there were still more clothes in the closet than I had ever owned in my entire life. I changed into a pair of black pants and tank top like the clothes the others were wearing in the training center. The material was soft and conformed to my body better than anything I had ever worn before. I took out the old clothes from my backpack and repacked it with as many sets of the new clothes as I could fit inside. Even though I had no intention of leaving but I wanted to be prepared just in case.

I stored my backpack in the far corner of the closet. I wanted to remind myself I had the choice to stay here or leave at any time. I knew I wasn't going to leave any time soon. Despite only being in the house for a few hours, I felt like I was home.

I was left on my own to explore once I had changed my clothes. Welhiem told me I was free to check out the house and wander around as much as I wanted. When I felt up to it, I was welcome to join them. The others were on the first floor in the training center. I could feel their energy as they worked through exercises they spent eons perfecting.

Memories of those skills flashed through my mind. It was difficult to wrap my head around the new skills my family had shared with me during our bonding. My brain told me I knew each movement, angle and position as clearly as if I had been practicing them for hundreds of years, but my body tripped over the ideas as if it was a newborn colt. I was confused more than anything else. When I feasted on human souls I could feel their experiences and live their memories, making them my own. But, humans lived such a short lifespan. Their experiences were not ingrained and drawn out like the Were. I wondered if this is what drove the other Were insane. A lifetime of experiences expanding well beyond my own bouncing around in my head would surely drive me mad, unless I found a way to control it.

I wasn't ready to join the others yet. Everything was all so new and overwhelming, I needed to take a break. I left my room and started exploring the hallways. At first, I wandered around the halls, heedless to where I was going. I opened doors at random, checking out the rooms at leisure. If a room caught my interest for more than a few moments I would go inside and explore, but overall there wasn't much to find inside.

At first, I kept my wandering to the second floor. I had already seen everything on the first floor and everyone was downstairs. I wanted a little bit of time before joining the others again, so I meandered around the second floor for a little while. The house was massive, spreading out with brightly lit rooms. I think I opened about a dozen doors exposing massive bedrooms, wide closets, cavernous bathrooms with soaker tubs, even a rec room with a pool table, mahogany bar and sitting areas like the ones in the living room downstairs. Everything in the room was centered on togetherness. A place to play, eat, talk and work together. The only rooms set up for anyone to be alone were the bedrooms and even those were spacious and had sitting areas for more than one person. All the bedrooms doors were left at least partially open almost as an invitation to walk inside. I wondered if these Were ever spent any time alone.

I had explored all the rooms in the three wings of the house, avoiding entering the obviously occupied rooms, and was contemplating heading downstairs when I noticed a door at the end of the hall. It was tucked back in an alcove and wasn't well-defined so I hadn't noticed it at first. It was the only completely closed door on the entire floor. I hesitated as I reached for the handle, considering the secrets this family may be hiding. I questioned the wisdom of opening unfamiliar doors, especially considering I had only been with the family for a few hours. My hand was on the handle, ready to turn the knob when I heard the light tread of footsteps in the hall behind me.

I could feel Darlene's presence even before she turned the corner of the hallway. Stepping back from the closed door I turned to leave, but Darlene rounded the corner before I moved too far. As soon as she saw me her face broke into a wide grin. I could tell she was once a beautiful woman, but age had softened her features, melting them into a mass of wrinkles and sagging skin.

"You can go up there." She nodded in the direction of the closed door since her hands were loaded down with a laundry basket overflowing with freshly laundered and folded towels. "We have nothing to hide here."

She moved into a bathroom, leaving me to contemplate the door. Hesitating just a moment more, I finally reached for the knob and turned it. I wasn't sure what I was expecting, but it definitely wasn't the brightly lit winding staircase leading to another floor.

My feet barely touched the steps as I sped to the next level in the house. I could almost feel the pull of the light drawing me to whatever was up there. The top of the staircase opened into a room spanning the entire length and breadth of the house. I could see areas of the room were dedicated to various activities, but for the most part the room was left open and unfurnished.

Bright sunlight flooded into the room from broad windows causing refracted light to bounce of wall-length mirrors and crystal light fixtures. The floor was a brightly polished and the pale hardwood seemed to glow with an inner light. Against the far wall the floor was covered with thick canvas and several artist easels were scattered in a lopsided circle. The opposite wall housed what looked like some type of recording equipment. A series of musical instruments were displayed against the walls or were resting in stands.

The only wall in the room was the glass enclosure housing the microphones and recording equipment. A short hallway led to an area behind the recording studio. My curiosity led me down the hallway first, but the only thing there was a small bathroom with little more than a toilet and a shower. I only gave a cursory glance to the musical instruments displayed against the wall. Music really held no interest for me.

I made my way across the open expanse of the room, doing a few flips in the middle. The openness of the area just seemed to call out for movement. As I tumbled I managed to catch a glimpse of myself in the mirrors lining the wall. It was hard to believe the long, lean form reflecting the grace filled angles and arches was me. I had never seen myself in motion and I was fascinated by the beauty of it. I stood in the center of the room for a while, twisting and turning and contorting my body into shapes I had never tried before. Even without shape-changing I was able to drastically change how I appeared many times over. I was tempted to change my shape to see the metamorphosis, but shape-change takes energy and, since I didn't know when I was going to be able to hunt again I needed to conserve what energy I had.

Glass windows covered one wall from floor to ceiling. The sun was warming huge squares of the hardwood floor and I was tempted to lay down and relish the warmth and energy from the radiant heat, but I wasn't exactly sure how the others would react to me sprawling out in the middle of the floor if they decided to come looking for me. Reluctantly, I turned from the warmth of the windows and moved across the room. The artists' easels each contained a canvas with paintings in various stages of completeness and obviously different skill levels. It was an art class interrupted and frozen in time.

A stack of canvases were piled against the wall. I wondered if they were more student pieces and I crouched down to go through them. The top layer had a few outlines in charcoal. I could see the beauty in the clean lines and shapes drawn on the canvas. These were obviously not student pieces.

As I sifted through the canvases I unburied more pieces. After the first layers I found some nearly completed paintings. I spread the canvases out, trying to see the story they told. By the time I was finished the canvases covered the floor from the artist easels all the way to the recording studio. I didn't know a lot about art, but I could see the beauty glowing from the canvases. Each painting represented a major event from human history. I recognized some of the scenes from the books Agnes had given me to read when I was in the asylum as a child. It was like I was looking at human history from the perspective of the artist. It was beautiful.

I did my best to put the paintings in order, but it was like trying to piece together a huge jigsaw puzzle with only half the pieces. It took about two hours to get them arranged to my satisfaction. Finally, I stood before my work, studying the faces and images glaring up at me.

The lines and symmetry of the paintings drew me to each image. Each one told a different story. Stories I was familiar with from the history books from Agnes' library, but there was something different about each one. The events were all clearly depicted. Images of the Salem Witch trials, pilgrims on the Mayflower, Queen Elizabeth's court, each painting depicted familiar scenes in minute detail.

I was about halfway through the paintings when I started to notice them. Sometimes they were in the background, sometimes they were right in the forefront of the pictures. Bright balls of lights floated through the scenes casting shadows and highlights against the faces in each painting.

I worked my way around to the beginning of the paintings. I knew the story. Living in a building attached to a convent forced it deeply into my brain. There were a couple of paintings I couldn't quite place. One was a dark, confusing mass of shadows with one, tiny bright spot growing from one corner with subtle rays spreading through the darkness. The other one was completely opposite. Bright light flooded the canvas, overwhelming the shadows. But the darkness was still there, hidden within the light.

I walked by six paintings, each one representing the six days of creation. And on the seventh day he rested. The painting representing the seventh day was a canvas dominated by a huge blue planet. Land masses peeked out of blue mists, hinting at the shapes of continents. Bright lights burst out from behind the planet like rays of the sun burning away shadows.

The Eden portrait was unmistakable. Rich images gazed from the canvas, eyes shining in the light. Eve stood in the midst of the garden surrounded by animals. The gentle curves of her body were unrestricted by clothing. Her skin was a pale, golden color with hints of pink on her nipples, cheeks and lips. She was so central in the image I didn't see the animals surrounding her at first. A lion with a reddish gold main leaned against her thigh. A bright-eyed peacock with his brightly colored tail on full display strutted in the background. Other animals were lying on the ground or grazing on green grass.

Despite all the details surrounding her, the image of Eve was so bright it was easy to see the artist was focused on her. A hand reached from the heavens offering a globe of bright light to the woman. Eve's hand reached out to accept the offering. There was no hesitation in her face, no questioning, just acceptance of the gift. I wondered if this was the artists attempt to represent the temptation of Eve.

The canvas was nearly as tall as I was and so wide I could barely stretch my arms across the surface.

I wanted to study the images closer so I propped the painting against the wall so I could see it better. I could hear the others stirring downstairs. My mind reached out to them, finding Stephen, Helena and Cassandra headed to their rooms. Darlene was in the kitchen. I could tell from her energy the kitchen was where she was the happiest. It took me a moment to locate Welhiem. I finally found him headed up the stairs to this room. Looking around I saw the canvases spread across the floor. I didn't have time to clean them up and put them back in place, so I just stood in the center of the room and waited for him to come.

Chapter Nineteen

I WATCHED AS THE door slowly opened and Welhiem stepped into the room. I prepared myself for the worst as he looked at the artwork spread across the floor.

He scanned the canvases and brought his eyes up to meet mine. A bright smile spread across his face and he gestured to the paintings.

"Stephen does beautiful work," he said. "You'll have to ask him about his inspiration."

I walked among the paintings, looking at them with a greater sense of respect. "What is this place?" I asked.

"This is really Helena and Cassie's place," he said. "I built this house for them. Helena finds herself in her music. She teaches lessons and helps young artists make demo tapes. Of course, she feeds on the energy of her students as they create."

"What does Cassandra do up here?" I looked at the parts of the shiny floor not covered by paintings.

"Cassie likes to dance," he said. "It keeps her out of trouble. We can't risk her teaching lessons to young ones, her appetites are too unique. Stephen has been offering painting lessons while he's been staying here, but we'll put those on the back burner until you get settled in. You'll have different needs from my other children and we are going to need to change a few of our hunting habits while you're here."

"You call her Cassie?" I asked.

"It's easier to get her attention when she's being playful." Father brushed his fingers through my hair and patted my cheek.

I wondered what kind of trouble Cassandra could get in to. She was a Were. One of the strongest I had ever met. I doubted there was anyone who could hurt Cassandra. Well, maybe Sebastian. He might be strong enough to take on a Were like Cassandra. For a moment my mind flashed on the Warrior I had met in the graveyard. He was another one who could possibly take on Cassandra.

"Let's put the paintings back for now," he said. Darlene has a meal prepared for us and we are going hunting tonight."

It only took the two of us a few minutes to put the paintings back where we found them. I tried to put them back in the order I decided they belonged. Surprisingly, Welhiem seemed to realize what I was attempting and helped me put them in order. I helped drape a heavy drop cloth over the paintings before we headed down to the dining room.

I was only a few steps behind him as we made our way down the stairs and through the house. He stopped at the top of the stairs leading down to the first floor and turned to face me.

"You have questions," he said. "Don't be afraid to ask, child. We don't have anything to hide."

There was no reproach in his eyes as he smiled at me. I knew he was being honest in his offer. I couldn't help but feel at ease and returned his smile.

"Will Stephen be angry at me for looking at the paintings?" I wasn't afraid of Stephen's reaction, but I was starting to feel like I belonged to this coven and I didn't want to offend my new brother.

"Of course not," Welhiem immediately smiled and wrapped his arm around my shoulder. "None of us are afraid of sharing our talents. He's not ready to show you everything, yet. Give him a little bit of time."

"He doesn't like me very much, does he?" I asked. All the other members of the family were so opened to me. Stephen seemed closed off compared to the others.

Welhiem stopped at the foot of the stairs, turning me to face him.

"Stephen was very hurt when Sebastian left us." His voice was low and gentle. "They were closer than brothers. It's just going to take time for him to come around."

It was hard to wrap my head around the creature I met in the dark alley being a member of this coven. Sebastian was so vicious and hungry. The desire to feed was strong in me. It was strong in all of us. But the hunger I felt in Sebastian was stronger than any need I had ever felt.

"Will we see Sebastian while we hunt?" I asked.

"It's always a possibility," Welhiem said. "This is a big city, but sometimes we tend to cross hunting grounds with other feeders. The others know I own the city. I allow them to hunt as long as they don't cross me and my children."

Father led me to the dining room. It had been quite a few hours since we had eaten and I wasn't hungry, but I knew better than to pass up food when it was offered. I could see the others taking their places at the table. Stephen pulled out chairs for Helena and Cassandra, allowing them to take their seats before moving to his own chair. They were strong. I could see their strength, even from this distance, but there were only three of them. In a city full of available prey, they had to be greatly outnumbered.

Stephen stood as soon as I entered the room and pulled a chair out for me. His smile was a little strained, but it didn't seem hesitant. As I sat down he placed his hand on my shoulder. He was warm and sweet. Darlene came in from the kitchen with a bowl of steaming rice. The table was filled with delicious looking food. I couldn't help noticing the lack of meat. Every dish Darlene offered up was completely vegetarian.

"You all didn't need to change your diet because of me." I took the bowl of rice Stephen handed me and started scooping some on to my plate.

"It wouldn't be the first time we went vegan." Helena smiled as she handed me a concoction of vegetables in a sweet sauce. "There are other members of our coven who don't eat meat."

I looked around at the others as they served up their food. None of them had refused the meat being served the day before.

"What do you mean?" I asked. "I didn't think any of you were vegan."

Welhiem smiled and patted my hand. "Oh, child. This isn't my entire coven. There are thousands of us scattered through this city and many more all throughout this world. My coven is the largest in the world, even bigger than your grandfather's."

"How do you know...?" I wasn't sure how to frame the question so I just left it hanging in the air between us.

"You have the markings of your family all around you." It was Cassandra who answered my question. Her smile was sweet and inviting. I sensed the cunning and strength behind her innocent looks, though. It was easy to see how she could seduce her prey into her web. "You'll learn to recognize the Were-bond. It takes time to see the markings. It's not an easy skill to teach because we all see energy a little differently."

I looked at each of the Were sitting at the table. Their energy was shining brightly, surrounding their forms. It took me a few moments to look through their energy and find the shapes inside them. I wasn't surprised to see the wolf hidden in everyone. I wondered if everyone in Welhiem's coven were wolves or if his pack adopted other Were creatures.

"What do you see when you look at us, child?" Welhiem's voice was gentle as he prompted me.

"You're all light. All over light. It surrounds you and radiates with different colors. And I can see shapes within the color." They all leaned in towards me as if they were being drawn in by my words. "Everyone is always surrounded by light. It's easy to find the light. It's the darkness hidden in the light that's sometimes hard to see."

Stephen locked eyes with me. I could see the question in his face, but instead of asking he shoveled a forkful of vegetables into his mouth. I just wished he would ask me and not leave the question hanging in the air. Living in the asylum didn't make me the best conversationalist. Most of the patients were trapped in their own little realm of reality where conversations based in reality rarely provided any mental stimuli.

The food was filling, at least for my body. I could feel the need for energy pulling at me. The light around the others was pulsing and spinning, ducking in and out of their bodies. I had never seen another

Were prepare for a hunt before. We all packed as much food into our bodies as we could handle. After dinner we all helped Darlene clear the table. She shooed us out of the kitchen so we gathered in the living room. I stood, watching the by-play between the four Were. They touched and spoke to each other with such ease. I don't remember ever being able to touch any other being with any such comfort and beauty.

Welhiem gestured for me to join the group. I allowed him to draw me into the circle of their arms. We huddled together in the white space, our shoulders touching, arms wrapped around each other. I leaned my head into the warmth of their light, drawing in the energy. We stood there for a long time, basking in their shared warmth.

I kept my eyes closed, even after the others dropped their arms from my shoulders. It took a moment to center myself and separate my own energy and emotion from my new family's thoughts. I think the others must have realized what I was going through because not one of them spoke while I stood there trying to compose myself. When I finally did open my eyes, I realized the others had moved away from me and all seemed occupied in doing their own thing. I knew it was an act. Stephen glanced up at me and gave me a slight grin.

"We're going to go after some easy targets tonight." Welhiem led us towards the front door. I hesitated slightly before turning to follow. "We all need to feed tonight so we need to hit some high population areas. Maria, I think you have the most desperate need so we'll find you something first."

I shook my head, unsure of how to voice my concern. Welhiem took my hand and guided me towards the door. I could feel the hesitancy in my steps as I moved towards him. He stopped and studied my face, peering into my eyes as he assessed my mood. I could feel his mind probing mine as he looked into my soul and read my emotions.

"What concerns you, child?" I could hear the echoes of centuries in his voice when he spoke like this. His tone was buried beneath the shadows of history and layered with knowledge and power. I was drawn to him, not because of the power he held, but because of the knowledge he could share with me.

I shook my head again, trying to clear my thoughts. There was no help for it. I needed to tell Welhiem.

"I've never hunted in a pack before." My voice was low, hesitant even. "I need to feed, but I don't want to get in the way. I think it would be better if I hunted alone."

Welhiem smiled. It was his turn to shake his head. "Don't worry, child. You won't be in the way. You might even learn something from us."

"Agnes taught me how to feed." It wasn't quite true. Agnes taught me to control my feeding, but I had been consuming the energy of those around me long before Agnes ever got a hold of me.

"She taught you to feed, yes," Welhiem said. "But she didn't teach you to hunt. I have a feeling you've been trying to maneuver through the hunt on your own. We can teach you to hunt better than you could even imagine."

The taste of his promise was in the air. My skin tingled with suppressed energy as I continued to peer into his eyes. He practically glowed with power as he continued to gaze at me. Drawing me into an embrace, he engulfed me with his warmth. The bond between me and the coven was strengthening by the moment. I couldn't leave them now if I tried.

"How will I know what to do?" I asked. "I could cause problems in the hunt."

"How did you know to follow me?" Welhiem replied. "How did you know I wouldn't harm you? How did you know you belonged to this family? You'll know what to do when the time comes."

Welhiem turned and led us out the door. The others circled me and we followed. Welhiem's energy was easy to follow. He lit up the night like a beacon. My tongue darted out, tasting the flavor of the night. It was a beautiful night for a hunt.

Chapter Twenty

THE LIGHT FROM A second-story window did little to brighten the dark alleyway, but I could still easily see the huddled forms tucked behind the dumpster. There were three of them, wrapped in blankets and tucked away from prying eyes. Even from my perch, three stories above them, I could smell the reek of alcohol and sweat. The heat from the day was slowly leaching from the pavement and a slight chill was settling into the air.

Father was crouched beside me. Somewhere in the last few hours I had stopped thinking about him as Welhiem and had started thinking of him as father. Helena and Cassandra were on the rooftop opposite us and Stephen was at the opening of the alley. A brick wall behind the three sleeping forms created a blind alley. I sensed Helena's smile more than saw it. Our prey wasn't going anywhere.

As if on a prearranged signal the light from the window went out, bathing the alley in darkness. We all struck at the same time. Helena and Cassandra had their prey pressed against the brick wall with their mouths each on the base of his throat. Cassandra's hand was pressing against his mouth so tightly I could see blood seeping between her fingers. Streams of red fluid dripped down his face and flowed into Cassandra's mouth. A gentle purr of satisfaction emanated from her throat as she feasted on the man. Father and Stephen had grabbed the woman. Stephen's mouth was pressed tightly against hers while father had ripped her shirt and had his mouth pressed against her chest just above her left breast.

My own prey woke with a start when I leapt on him. A scream gurgled in his throat, trapped by the haze of alcohol and my legs crushing his rib cage. His dark brown eyes reflected fear as I pressed my lips against his full, broad mouth. He struggled against me so I grasped his head in my hands, my fingers sliding into his thickly matted hair. Vermin skittered away from my fingers, repulsed by the smell of my blood. I knew my blood was different than humans. Human blood carried oxygen and nutrients throughout their bodies. My body fed on energy, relying on a fraction of oxygen and nutrients of humans, making my blood thin and nearly purple in color. The vermin found me less than desirable and I knew they wouldn't find any purchase in my skin. I tightened my grip on the man's head and pressed my mouth harder against his. He moaned as his soul fled from his body into mine.

My kiss was gentle as I slowly drew his energy out of his body. I tasted his fear and self-loathing and I realized I wasn't the worst demon he had ever faced. Glimpses of jungles and firestorms flashed across my mind and the faces of boys, barely more than children, dying from injuries inflicted by weapons created by the hands of the most twisted souls of man burned through my soul. It was almost with a sigh of relief that he released his last breath from his body. As the last of his energy entered me I relaxed the grip of my legs and pushed away from his body. His dark eyes glazed over and his face relaxed into a near peaceful repose. Leaning over, I gently closed his eyes. He almost looked like he was asleep.

My whole body quivered as I processed the energy and stored it away. I knew the seizure was coming and I knew it was going to be bad. My brain was on fire. I felt arms wrap around me as I fell and suddenly the ground dropped from under me and I was staring at the night sky.

I slowly came back to myself. It took me a few moments to realize I was in a bed wrapped in soft, warm sheets with a cold compress across my eyes. I could feel the weight of bodies sitting on either side of me. One of them was gently stroking my cheek and brushing my hair away from my face. They were whispering to each other. I'm sure I wasn't meant to hear what they were saying.

"It happens sometimes when the child isn't taught to store the energy properly." It was father's voice. "She's more powerful than any Were I've ever taught. Her instincts are strong, but she needs to learn to use her gift. I just hope the damage isn't too deeply ingrained inside her. I don't think Agnes intended her to live this long. If she had succeeded in possessing this child there would be no stopping her."

"Your sister is becoming more powerful every generation." Darlene's voice was overshadowed with hate and anger. "We have to stop her before she taints any more lives."

Father hissed his disapproval. "That evil is no sister of mine. We may have been born together, but she has perverted her heritage beyond all recognition. I choose my own family and right now I choose this child. I'm going to do everything in my power to cure her and bring her back to herself."

I reached up to remove the compress covering my eyes. Father smiled as my eyes met his. It was obvious he had known I was awake and had intended for me to hear the conversation.

"Do you feel better, child?" he asked.

Nodding my head, I attempted to sit up in the bed. Darlene adjusted the pillows behind my back and smoothed the blankets over my legs, patting my knee when she finished. Neither of them moved from where they were sitting. The energy from my feeding had settled into place and I could feel strength coursing through my body.

"You're a thing of beauty, child," father said. "I've never seen anyone feed as well as you."

"I bet you've never seen anyone seize as bad as I did either." I tried to make it sound like a joke, but my voice cracked halfway through my words.

"Actually," his mouth twisted into a sardonic smile. "It's not as uncommon as you may think. Especially in young Were who develop their feeding skills early."

"Agnes told me I developed my abilities early." I said. "It confused me though. I thought we were all born with the ability to feed."

Father reached up and smoothed my brow. "We are, but most of us are latent feeders until we become adults in what humans would call their teen years. Learning to feed properly is a rite of passage amongst our kind. You've been a full-fledged feeder since birth, if I read your energy right. Something must have happened to you when you were born to do this to you."

I shuddered as the memory of the witch and her blood woke my senses and forced the images into my mind. Swallowing the bile rising in my throat, I shook my head to try to displace the disturbing images.

"How do others learn to feed if they aren't born with the knowledge?" I asked. Father seemed willing to teach me and from what little I've heard I probably had a lot to learn.

"Most of our kind are born into Covens or, at the very least, into extended families of Were-creatures." His voice was gentle and seemed full of regret as he spoke. I wondered if he was thinking of my past or if there was some great regret and sorrow in his life. "Not every one of our kind become full-fledged feeders. Most are latent feeders and can feed on the bits of energy humans bleed off during the course of their daily lives. Only a handful of true feeders are born every generation."

"What does it mean to be a full-fledged feeder?" I thought about the number of feeders living in Portland and the few feeders I had met here. There seemed to be an excessive number of feeders around for this to be true.

"A true feeder can drain the entire life-force from a human quickly on his or her own." Father said. "Some latent feeders are strong and when they team up with others they can drain the entire life-force of a human, especially if the human is weakened due to illness or injury."

There were more questions bubbling up inside of me. The more I learned the more I wanted to know. I was coming to realize Agnes had only been feeding me enough information about my abilities to keep me compliant with her own desires. This man, the man whom after just a few hours I was already referring to as father, had no such interest in me. Every ounce of his energy was focused on teaching me what I needed to know to become what I was born to be. The questions filled my mind, running over each other and twisting in my head until they became a giant, incoherent mass. It took me a few moments to sort through them all to pull out the one I really needed the answer to the most.

"What are we? I read all the legends and know how the humans view us, but where did we come from?" I wasn't sure if I was making much sense, but I kept trying. "I want to know the reality behind the legend."

Father leaned forward and patted my hand. "Everything we know about what we are has been passed down through legend and myth, just like human knowledge." He must have sensed my disappointment in his answer because he leaned forward and rubbed my shoulder as if to soothe me. "Of course, many of us are so long lived we may actually remember our creation." I gave him a courtesy smile, knowing he was expecting me to laugh at his joke. "I guess I could tell you my favorite version of where we came from."

I actually gave him a genuine smile this time. I don't know how much of what he was going to tell me was real, but maybe it would satisfy some of my curiosity.

"The earliest legends of our time teach us we originated as pure energy. We grew in knowledge and ability and soon outgrew our energy forms." His tone and mannerism changed as he spoke and I got the impression he had told this story many times. "Some of our kind tried to join with creatures on this earth, but the bond between the lesser creatures and the Were was tenuous at best. It wasn't until humans came into existence that we found our true match. Some say it was actually a Were who tempted Eve in the garden and the first fruit of her womb was an unearthly creature. I don't know how the first one of our kind came into existence, but however it happened he was a blend of the earthly mortal creatures and a being of pure energy. Legends tell of this phenomenon happening many different times. The children of the mortal creature and the gods always have remarkable abilities beyond any mortal comprehension."

I remembered the stories I read when I was in the asylum. Children of gods with powers gifted to them by their other-worldly parents always fascinated me with their adventures. I wondered if the stories were actually based on Were-creatures or if they were just myths and legends based on man's imagination.

"I feel like there's so much to learn." I said. "Agnes didn't teach me much."

Father smiled gently and rubbed my shoulder. "We'll have plenty of time," he said. "I'm sure you want to rest and spend some time meditating. The others should be finished taking care of the bodies by now and will be home soon. Come join us in the training room when you're ready." He left me after one more pat on the shoulder.

The bed was soft, too soft. I couldn't focus on drawing my energy into my core. Finally, I got out of bed and headed upstairs to the attic. I could feel Cassandra's energy spinning around even before I made it to the top step. Music was playing so loud the windows were vibrating. I stood enthralled as she danced across the floor, spinning, flipping, twirling and turning as she flashed around the space. She knew I was there. I could feel her energy reaching out to me, drawing me into her light. I crossed the threshold into the room. At first, I just watched, but her movements were an invitation. I crossed to the center of the room and started to dance with her. I lacked her grace. My movements were stiff and more reminiscent of martial arts moves, but I was dancing. As we moved Cassie gave me gentle prodding and soon I lost myself in the dance.

Chapter Twenty-one

WHEN WE FINISHED CASSIE threw her arms around me and kissed me on the top of my head. Her laughter surrounded me, filling me with strength and energy. We went down the stairs together and walked down the hall to our rooms. Neither of us spoke. We didn't need to, everything was said in the quiet of our minds. She left me in the doorway of my room, letting me know she would be waiting for me with the others. I showered and changed, tossing my soiled clothes into the hamper. My family was waiting for me when I made my way down to the training room.

I could see the change in their energy as soon as I walked into the room. They all glowed brighter, as if a switch had been turned on inside of their bodies. Stephen and Helena were stretching and practicing backflips across the room. Cassandra ran across the room and wrapped her arms around Stephen. Releasing him, she stretched out on her back, her arms and legs sprawled as wide as they could reach. The others flipping over her body as if she wasn't even there.

Cassandra rolled to her feet with a flip, turning to the others with a quick grin. She quickly became a whirling blur as she too began to flip and twist around the room. I could tell she was faster and better than the others as she made her way around the broad, open space. Light burst from her, streaking through the room, following her as she danced around the room. She was like a firefly, lighting up the night and pulsing her seductive call throughout the room. I watched, enthralled by her beauty.

I heard a whistle behind me and turned to find father walking into the room. The others came to a complete standstill, their lights drawing into their bodies. Despite their complete stillness the room still vibrated with repressed energy. It was only when they were completely still that I could see them as they truly were. Helena and Cassandra looked more like sisters than mother and daughter. I knew they were hundreds of years old, yet they looked no older than I did at nineteen. Their look was too similar to not have a genetic connection and I didn't see the reflection of hundreds of conquered souls in their light like I did Agnes'. Somehow, they had learned to keep their youth and beauty better than Agnes. I wondered if I could learn their trick.

I turned to father and extended my hand to him. I realized I craved the physical connection between me and the other Were. My hand was so dim in comparison to my father's light. My body burned with the energy I had consumed, yet my own energy didn't glow nearly as bright as the others. Father brushed my forehead with his fingers, gently pushing my wet hair back from the top of my eyebrows.

"Why do you keep your hair so short, child?" He asked. "Helena's and Cassandra's hair doesn't interfere with their hunt."

"My hair just doesn't grow very fast." I rubbed my hand across my scalp, forcing my hair to spike up around my head. "It's so thin and patchy I don't even bother with it."

"And your blood? Is it also so thin?" He smiled when I nodded my response. "You're probably one of the most pure-blood Were I've met in centuries. It's unfortunate you weren't raised with knowledge of your abilities."

"Was Agnes such a bad teacher?" I asked. "Did I not learn anything? You saw me feed. I think I learned enough to at least survive."

"Yes, child," he said. "You learned to survive, but did you learn to thrive?"

Bowing my head, I contemplated his question. I seemed to do well enough for myself. I always had enough food to eat and could easily find shelter when I needed it. Thriving wasn't on the top of my list of necessities. In the streets the only thing that really mattered was survival.

"I can feel the energy you consumed flowing through your body, but it's fading too fast," he explained. "You need to learn to meditate and store your energy so it's there when you need it."

"Agnes showed me how to meditate." I thought back to the first few months in the Asylum and how Agnes would spend hours kneeling beside me as we slowly chanted the Latin words that really didn't mean anything to us but disguised what we were really doing. "I can calm my thoughts and allow the energy to settle."

"But, does the energy go where you need it or does it just follow the path of least resistance and settle wherever it wants."

"I don't understand." I said. "Agnes didn't tell me anything about storing energy."

"She wouldn't," he said. "Agnes was always impatient and greedy. She never took the time to learn how to properly meditate. The concept of conserving energy was always beyond her. My sister doesn't have the gift of discernment when it comes to selecting her prey either. To her the whole world is her smorgasbord and humans are the offerings."

"Aren't they, though?" I asked. "We are designed to feast on the energy of humans. Why should we discriminate between our preys? Do humans discern between the cow and the chicken or the pig and the goat? It's all food to them."

Father took both of my hands in his and turned me so I was looking into his eyes. He dropped my hands and cupped my face in his hands. The energy in his fingers tickled my cheeks and awoke my senses. I savored the taste of his soul as he inched into my mind.

"Do you really believe every human soul is ours for the taking?" The words were spoken so softly I almost didn't understand the question. It took me a moment to realize he didn't speak the words out loud. He spoke them directly to my mind.

My entire body quivered. There was pressure behind my eyelids, but I knew I wouldn't cry. I controlled my emotions; my emotions didn't control me. Biting my lip, I gave my head a tiny shake.

"Agnes didn't care whose soul she takes," I said. "And the others, the ones living on the streets, the only thing they cared about was making sure they didn't get caught."

I never thought about how I choose my victims. I knew I couldn't take souls just because the opportunity was there. When I hunted I sought out pain. Those in pain deserved release. And those who inflicted pain, the ones who caused darkness, they deserved death. I couldn't bring myself to feed indiscriminately, like Agnes. There was always plenty of pain out there for me to feast upon.

"What about you?" He asked. "What motivates your hunt?"

I couldn't put my thoughts into words. Hunting fulfilled a need. In order to survive I needed to consume energy and the humans provided the energy I needed. But to kill, just because I could. It was unconscionable to feed so indiscriminately. I never did understand Agnes' need to feed on any soul within her grasp.

Father dropped his hands from my face and reached out for me. I placed my hands in his, feeling the energy flow from the center of my body to the tips of my fingers. "I think you know what makes me and my sister different. Just because we have the ability to do something doesn't mean we should."

I closed my eyes and allowed his warmth to flow from my fingertips and flood through my body. We stayed engulfed in each other's energy and I savored the strength I received from him. There was a different quality to his energy. It was warm, especially when compared to Agnes' cold hardness.

"Does that knowledge make us any less evil, father?" I asked. "Just because a monster has a conscience doesn't make it righteous."

"Who determines right and wrong, child?" He asked. "Do we hold ourselves to the human's values or do we make our own rules?"

I turned and looked at the others. They had continued in their exercises while father and I had been talking. Stephen and Helena were involved in a battle royal involving weapons they had taken from the wall. They moved much faster than even I could imagine. Cassandra swirled around them like a beacon, highlighting the flash of steel and the ring of metal as the two fought. They were perfectly matched. Neither of them were able to get the hand up on the other. I watched the dance of light as they circled and spun around the room.

"It's beautiful, isn't it?" Father's eyes followed the battle as the two continued to fight. "Are you interested in learning to fight like them?"

"Why would I need to learn to fight?" Despite my confusion I was drawn to the battle. "I'm stronger than any human. I don't need to learn to fight in order to feed."

"No, but there are other creatures out there besides humans," father replied. "We must learn to defend ourselves against those who would destroy us."

"I know there are those who would hunt us." I said. "I've been hunted, but I managed to get away." I didn't mention the priest and his role in my escape. "What are these creatures?"

"Their origins are as obscured in myth as much as the beginnings of ours and the humans' existence are hidden in the mists of time." We continued to watch the flashes of light as Helena and Stephen fought, weapons flashing in the light. "Perhaps I'll tell you some of the stories one day."

I tried to keep the disappointment off my face, but father must have sensed my emotions. He took my arm under the elbow and led me outside. The warmth of the sun caressed my cheeks and strengthened my core.

"I think, maybe, I can tell you a few of the stories now," he said. "Come, let us find a place to talk. Then you'll meditate."

We walked outside into the sunlight. The warmth of the sun was nothing compared to the warmth radiating from my father. He led me to the tallest, widest rock in the yard. It was easily the height of ten men and as wide as the bed of a semi-truck. With one leap he landed on the top of the stone and gestured for me to follow. There was no way I could make the leap as effectively as father so I scrambled up the face, clinging to the hollows in the rock face with my fingers.

The top of the rock was unnaturally smooth, providing a perfect place to sit and talk. Father was already sitting by the time I made my way to the top. He motioned for me to sit across from him. I eased myself into the same cross-legged position as he was, resting my arms on my legs   "I always find it so restful up here," father said. "There's nothing between me and my thoughts but the stone and the sky."

I peered up at the clear, blue sky uninterrupted by clouds. A breeze scattered sand around the stone playground, but we were high enough off the ground to not be affected by it.

"I think you'll find it easy to meditate up here," he said. I nodded my approval. I always found being outside much more preferable to being enclosed inside, no matter how luxurious the surroundings.

"Now, you wanted to learn about the Warriors?" I leaned forward, anticipating the opportunity to learn about the man who so easily killed three Were and then turned his attention to me. "Our kind has been a part of the human tradition for as long as humans have been telling stories. I suppose the Hunters and the Warriors have been around as well."

I jerked my head up when he mentioned Hunters. The Warrior species made sense to me, at least in the limited knowledge of had of them. I wanted to learn more about the Hunter species. If the priest was going to be hunting me down I wanted to learn as much about him as I could. Agnes had been remiss in my education about the creatures sharing our realms and I wanted to be prepared when the Hunter and Warrior tracked me down again.

"Ah, yes." Father spoke quietly. "Agnes truly has been remiss in your education. If you don't learn about the Hunters and the Warriors you will be doomed to certain death."

Chapter Twenty-Two

I FACED DEATH MANY times in my life. Most of the time I was the one dealing out the death card. I could count on one hand the number of times I faced my own mortality. No, I take that back. I could count on one finger the time I faced my own death. It seemed ironic it took place in the same graveyard where I had been found on the day of my birth. I needed to learn about these creatures who held my death in their hands.

"You shield yourself from me, child." Father reached forward and grabbed my hands. "You don't need to fear my judgment. Tell me what happened when you met the Warrior."

I studied my hands cupped in his. He was holding my hands palms up and I could see the lines crisscrossing the soft flesh, telling the story of my life, as short as it was. I curled my fingers to cover my palms but didn't draw away from his grasp.

"My grandfather had sent three of his lackeys to recruit me." My voice was soft, but steady as I told the story. "They tracked me down to a little graveyard beside a church. I managed to get away but was still close enough to see them get hunted down and slaughtered by what I suppose was a Warrior. When he killed them, their bodies turned to dust and great balls of energy rose up and entered the Warrior's body. I didn't think he saw me, but when I turned to leave another man was there." I paused. A sudden realization about the role of the priest drew me up short. I had to learn more about the Hunter species. I could understand the Warrior. He and I were just extensions of the same creature. The Hunter had a power I couldn't understand.

It took me a moment to formulate my thoughts. I wasn't sure if I could explain what happened to me. "He forced me to walk to where the Warrior was standing." I struggled with the words. "He held me there and the Warrior would have slaughtered me but the two started arguing. While they were distracted I managed to get away. That's when I decided to come here."

"I can't fault you for your choice, child." He released my hands, allowing me to drop my hands back into my lap. "To be hunted is quite an unsettling prospect. I'm afraid once a Hunter has locked in on you it's impossible to shake them. He has your scent now and he will hunt you until either you're dead or he is."

The tension coiling in my chest grew, driving deep into my core. From the moment I faced the Warrior
I knew I was facing my death. Father was just confirming what I already knew. Now I knew I also had to worry about the Hunter creature as well.

"Will he find me here?" I asked.

"Here, somewhere else," he said. "It doesn't matter. He'll find you. You can try to run and hide, or you can stand and fight."

My hands curled into fists where they rested against my legs. I could feel my muscles tense as I anticipated the fight ahead. Biting my lip, I tried to hide the smile creeping onto my face.

"I'm not afraid of a fight." I said.

Father took my face in his hands and leaned forward, brushing his lips against my forehead. "None of us are," he said. "We've all been hunted at one point or another. Some of us more than once. As far back as recorded history we have been at war with the Hunters and the Warriors."

"War?" I needed clarification. The library at the asylum held many history books and I was familiar with the concept of war. There wasn't a time in human history untouched by war. But, humans waged war with weapons and words. I had a feeling the war between Were and Hunters was fought on a different level. "How do we wage war when we don't have any weapons?"

"We're not human soldiers. We don't require projectiles and armor carried in shielded caravans led by tanks." There was a slight trace of humor in the base of his words as he explained. "Our battleground is on a far different plain."

The sun had warmed the surface of the stone to a pleasant temperature. I could feel the heat rumbling in waves across the desert as the breeze increased in strength. Drawing in a deep breath, I allowed the energy from the warm breeze to fill my body. My heartbeat was slowing and my breathing was becoming shallower. I was almost ready to enter my meditative state, but I wanted to learn more about the Hunters. This time I leaned forward and placed my hand on father's arm.

"Who are the Hunters?" I asked. "Where did they come from?"

Father stood up and reached for me. He helped me to my feet before stretching out his back. "I'm getting too old to sit on a rock for a long time."

He shook out his legs, bending and stretching. I didn't feel any ill effects from sitting, but I did take a few minutes to stretch. He motioned for me to sit before he again took his position facing me.

"The histories don't give us a clear beginning of our kind," he explained. "Some of the histories say all humanity used to be like us, able to draw on energy around us to change shape and live for centuries. Time and evolution took its toll on the human race. Life spans were shortened. They're now trapped in one form, unable to assume another shape. And, most tragically, are unable to use the energy found all around them to survive. All of their energy must come from the food they take into their bodies."

"I still need to eat," I wasn't very hungry, but I knew Darlene was preparing the evening meal for us.

"There are no pure Were-creatures in the world any longer," father said. "Of course, no one knows our true origin so we don't know if there ever have been creatures capable of living on pure energy. Some stories say the Hunters, Warriors and Were all came from the same tribe and we all split many eons ago. Others say we all evolved independently, from rival tribes, and have been battling each other since the earth first formed, or even before in other incarnations."

The sun had moved and I could feel my entire left side becoming overly warm. I shifted slightly to position myself more directly in the sun's rays. Father reclined, stretching out his legs and resting on his elbows. I thought about stretching out, but I was afraid I would drop into a meditative state if I relaxed too much.

"What's the difference between the tribes then?" I asked. "If we all started the same wouldn't we all have the same abilities?"

"Are your abilities the same as mine, or Cassandra's, or even Stephen's?" He asked. "Every one of us have different abilities, different talents. The Hunters and Warriors are similar to our kind, but their abilities diverged from ours and they became our sworn enemies. At first, we were three tribes all battling the others, but a truce was made between the Hunters and the Warriors. We are now one tribe against two, battling each other in the dark corners and secret places of this world."

My mind returned to the graveyard where I first met the Warrior. The priest had to have been a Hunter, but he seemed so confused when he met me I seriously doubted he knew what he was. I needed to learn more about these creatures, especially since it seemed they had latched on to me and were hunting me down.

"What do they feed on if not human energy?" I asked.

"I think you know the answer to that one, child." Father brushed the hair off my forehead.

The light I saw traveling from the Were killed by the Warrior's weapon and entering his body told me how he fed. I was still confused about the priest, though. He seemed confused by what he saw in the graveyard. If he had been raised in the tribes, as father said most of our kind were, he would have been able to identify me and the Warrior. He had mentioned being raised in an orphanage. I wondered if Agnes had taken him from his kind before he learned what he was. For every question father answered twenty more filled my head. I had a feeling we were just scratching the surface of the history of our kind.

"Agnes used to give me books to read when I had questions," I said. "Maybe if you give me some books on Hunters and Warriors I will be able to learn on my own."

Father chuckled before standing up and stretching again. "We don't have a written history of our kind, child," he said. "Some things need to remain secret. Our enemies already have great power. If they knew our secrets we would be easier to hunt."

"Agnes has books about our kind." I knew this conversation was going to end soon. I was starting to slip into a daze. It wouldn't be long before I dropped into a full meditative state.

Father crouched, looking into my eyes. "Agnes is impatient and careless. Most of her books are written by Hunters and Warriors. She has a few written by our kind, but she usually keeps them close by, sharing them only with those she intends to kill."

I dropped my head, bringing my chin nearly to my chest. "She tried to kill me." I think what she tried to do to me was worse than death. If she had succeeded in taking over my body I would have been trapped inside of her, consumed by her ever-growing hunger.

"I have no doubt she did." Father said. "Now, you are nearly ready to drop. Would you like me to teach you a meditative technique so you can better store energy?"

I nodded and started to stand. He gestured for me to stay down. I stretched out on the rock, resting my head on my arms. The warmth of the sun bathed my face with its rays. Closing my eyes, I allowed my other senses to take over, drawing on the voice of the desert. I could feel the energy of my earlier feasting buzzing in my head. Father was watching me. I could feel his eyes studying my face as I slipped deeper into my meditative state.

"Maria, child, can you hear me?" He asked.

I nodded, but I was too deep into my trance to respond to his questions vocally. He removed my hands from under my head, placing something soft between me and the stone. He removed my jacket and shoes, leaving me only in the tank top and shorts I had put on after my shower.

"Relax, child." He brushed his hands through my hair, touching my face and working his way down to my shoulders. "Feel the touch of my hands. I will guide the energy to the strongest areas of your body. When you feel the touch of my hands allow the energy to flow and reside there."

His hands left my body as his words penetrated my consciousness. Soothing, lulling me into peacefulness. His hands returned, this time resting on the top of my head. As soon as he touched me I could feel the warmth of my energy rushing to my crown. His hands rested on the top of my head for a few moments before moving to my forehead. As the energy traveled down I could feel residual energy at the crown of my head, causing my hair to stand on end.

His fingers brushed my lips, bringing the energy into my mouth. He paused only briefly before bringing his hands to the pulse points on my neck, exerting gentle pressure to the gently, throbbing veins. His hands trailed across my shoulders and rested on my chest, just above my left breast. The strength of the blood coursing through his veins throbbed against my heart. The energy burned a trail to meet the throbbing.

I was barely aware of his touch. My breathing was even and shallow and my heartbeat was slowing. Father's hands trailed down my body, resting briefly above my navel and a little longer on my pelvic crest. His fingers barely brushed my legs before coming to rest on the soles of my feet. My entire body tingled with the stored energy. The desert lulled me into complacency and I allowed myself to slip into deep meditation. I wasn't even aware of Father leaving me to my rest.

Chapter Twenty-Three

THE SMELL OF BLOOD was so strong I could almost taste the metallic tang on my lips. My eyes flew open and I sat up, trying to control the retching feeling from deep in my gut. I was still on the rock with the desert sun warming my skin. The sun had dipped closer to the horizon. Nearly three hours had passed while I was lost in meditation. Cassandra was perched on my left just inches from where I had been resting. She smiled up from where she was reclining

I pulled myself to my feet, brushing bits of sand and grit from my clothing. My exposed skin nearly glowed in the bright afternoon light. No amount of sun would ever change the color of my skin. Not even a slightly darker tone to denote the hours I spent under the rays of the eye of heaven. Cassandra stood with one graceful motion. She stood on her toes, spinning until she was only a few inches from my face. Her skirt flared out, brushing against my arms. My breath caught in my throat as the smell of blood permeated the air. I could feel the edge of the rock at my heels as she forced me back. I stopped, refusing to let her push me over the edge. For a moment we stood there, facing each other, eyes locked.

"Cassandra!" Father's voice was sharp and filled with reprimand. "Leave her alone! Get down here, child."

Cassandra tipped her head and smiled at me. Father was talking to her, not me. She stepped away and looked down over the edge of the rock. I moved to stand beside her, standing far enough away so when

I held my breath I didn't have to smell her. Father was standing at the base of the stone, Stephen and Helena stood behind him.

"I'm just playing, Father." I knew Cassandra was hundreds of years old, yet the slight whine in her voice reminded me of the young, pubescent girls I grew up with in the foster homes. The tone grated on my ears, causing the muscle between my shoulder blades to twinge.

"Our new sister is not familiar with your games, Cassandra." Helena's voice was gentle as she coaxed her daughter to descend from the rock. "There will be time enough to play once Maria learns the rules."

Cassandra backed away from the edge of the rock. She reached the far side of the tower and crouched low. I wasn't sure what her plan was, but it looked like she needed a little room. I moved to a corner of the rock and settled my center of gravity. If she suddenly changed direction I wanted to be prepared. I could see the others below me looking up at us. Father smiled at us and motioned for Cassandra to come down.

The tower was at least eight feet across. There was plenty of room for both of us to maneuver comfortably. Cassandra sprang forward, her feet barely touching the surface of the stone. When she reached the edge of the rock she pushed herself off, flinging herself into the air. Her dress spun around her, cocooning her body in purple silk before furling out in the wind. Her body twisted, nearly floating in the space between the top of the tower and the ground. She landed only inches from her mother, her feet barely disturbing the earth.

Father's smile was clear, even from this far away. The others were not as expressive, their emotions hidden behind blank masks. "You can come down now, Maria." Father gestured for me to join him.

I'm sure I could have made the leap safely to the ground, but there was no way I could do it with as much grace and beauty as Cassandra. Instead, I lowered myself over the edge and scrambled to the ground. Father put his arm around my shoulder and turned me towards the house.

"How was your meditation?" he asked.

I took a deep breath, taking stock of how I felt. My energy surged through me faster than I had ever felt it before. Every inch of my body was buzzing with the charge running through me. Cassandra danced past me, bringing with her the smell of blood. Covering my mouth and nose was completely reflexive. I didn't even notice I did it until the others turned and stared at me. We all stood in the center of the dusty field, surrounded by stone, staring at each other. Dropping my hand, I took shallow breaths trying to breathe through my mouth as much as possible.

"What's wrong, child?" Father's eyes narrowed, reflecting deep concern.

I stood still, afraid to move, afraid to talk. I couldn't say the scent of my new sister made me ill. There was no reason for her to smell so strongly of blood. Her clothes and skin seemed clean. I had been in close contact with her before and she didn't smell like this. It was like she bathed in blood.

Father made a motion with his hand, gesturing for the others to proceed into the house. He waited until they had disappeared into the house before turning back to me. "What's going on, child?" He asked again.

I swallowed back the bile in my throat, trying to rid my mouth of the bitter taste. "I can't describe it." I whispered.

Father placed his hand on my head, brushing my hair back and gently rubbing my scalp. "You do not need to fear me, child," he said. "You can tell me the truth."

My head was filled with the taste of blood and I couldn't speak through the flood of images in my brain. Pain wracked my body, forcing me to my knees. Father followed me to the ground. He wrapped his arms around me, cradling me in his warmth. My muscles tensed at the embrace, resisting the strength he was offering.

"Let me in, Maria," he whispered in my ear. "I can help you."

The flickers of his mind brushed my own, probing for entrance. He was searching for an opening into my memories. I could feel the vastness of his mind as he caressed my thoughts. His energy reached into me like fingers prodding my secrets. If I just reached into his mind I would have access to the knowledge of a thousand lifetimes. My mind reveled in the power he offered me, but I knew if I took his memories from his mind my senses would be so overwhelmed I wouldn't be able to process the knowledge. I could feel him pushing and opening the doors in my mind. My hidden places were being stripped bare and my secrets were being revealed.

Father slipped beyond the barriers I had spent my entire life hiding behind. He played through my memories as if he was watching a movie in fast forward, pausing at the events he found most interesting. I didn't want to live through those memories again. As he filtered through my history I could feel his reactions to the most remarkable events of my life. I shuddered as he replayed my harrowing birth and the awakening of my consciousness. I was expecting him to pull back in disgust when tasted the blood, but instead all I felt from him was sympathy.

Rage filled him when he saw my foster father enter my room. I could feel his body tremble as he watched the assault and the gentle brush of satisfaction as he watched the man die. He relived every soul I ever feasted on, tasting the sweetness of the energy as I once did. I had forgotten how many there were. Dozens, maybe even hundreds of humans, dead at my hands. I shared with him the pain each one inflicted on me. Each soul I had feasted upon was tainted with their own sins and, as I feasted, their sins became mine.

Agnes tainted all my memories from the moment my full powers manifested. She was the one who showed me where I could draw energy from the soul of my prey. She was the one who taught me to meditate. She was the one who taught me to store the energy of my prey to draw upon it later. Through my entire life she was the only one who had truly provided for me and yet her betrayal was so complete I knew I could never trust her again.

Father released me, allowing me to slip to the ground. I landed face down in the dirt, but father rolled me over before I inhaled a face full of gritty sand. With gentle fingers he brushed the dirt off my face and from my hair and then helped me sit up. He placed his arm around my back to steady me. I was grateful for the support because without it I would have probably collapsed in the dirt again.

"I'm so sorry, child," he whispered. "I needed to know what was causing you so much pain. I understand now."

My body quivered as we huddled together there in the dirt. I could feel the sickness I always felt after a seizure although I hadn't blacked out.

"What did you do to me?" I asked.

"I touched your soul and learned your history," he explained. "It is a gift many of us have, albeit to different degrees. I can absorb the life history of any soul I choose, but the toll is great. We will both need to feed tonight."

Twice in two days. I could usually go three or four days without feeding, sometimes longer if I conserved my energy and was able to absorb enough latent energy to keep me going. I usually only feed sooner when prey was easily available and I was unsure of when I would be able to hunt again.

I pulled myself to my feet, allowing father's arm to steady me. "Why?" It was all I could think to ask.

"You are ill, child," his voice was soft as he offered the explanation. "You were awakened long before you should have been and what Agnes taught you, or rather didn't teach you, further damaged your soul. You are powerful, perhaps the most powerful Were I have ever known, but you don't know how to control your power. That's why your body seizes when you consume energy. You can't control how the power enters your body and it floods in, overwhelming your senses. Our children are taught control from the time they are born. If we had been the one to find you we

176

might have been able to reverse the damage done to you by your birth. It is unfortunate Agnes found you first. I should have paid more attention to my sister's doings."

My body had finally stopped shaking and I was able to take a few, unsteady, steps on my own. Although my strength was coming back, I knew I need to replenish my energy soon.

"Will the others join us in our hunt?" I asked.

Father shook his head. "It will just be the two of us tonight," he answered. "The others won't need to feed for at least a few weeks, unless they end up doing something strenuous. Even then latent feeding should be enough to keep them satisfied. Besides, Helena needs to have a conversation with Cassandra about controlling certain appetites while you are a guest in our home."

When we made it to the house the others had disappeared. I could hear faint music coming from far above us and wondered if they were in the art room, as I had decided to call the artist's floor. Father directed me to go change into a hunting outfit so we could leave before the others came downstairs. I was sure they would know where we were going, even if father didn't tell them. My family had ways of communicating with each other beyond the spoken word.

Chapter Twenty-Four

I WAS SURPRISED WHEN father led me to the heart of the Las Vegas Strip. I would have thought he would bring me to a dark alleyway or a violent bar in the middle of a crime-ridden neighborhood. I knew there were many ways to find prey so to go unnoticed. If we hunted in the heart of the city it would be hard to hide the results. When bodies of dead tourist start to show up, or people who mattered suddenly disappear, the media tends to get up in arms and starts to dig into crime and murder statistics. It happened in Portland when the feeding frenzy was at its highest. I was pretty sure it would happen here, too.

We pushed through the crowds, forcing our way past families watching the shows outside of casinos, college students chugging alcohol from plastic containers nearly as tall as they were and tourists with cameras snapping photographs of everything bright and shiny all down the Strip. Energy buzzed through the air and I tasted as much of it as I could. Father walked slow enough I was easily able to touch the tourists at will and draw energy into my body.

My clothing was the most comfortable I had ever worn. The soft, grey pants were made to fit snuggly around my body yet move with me no matter what physical activity I was performing. My shirt was grey, sleeveless cotton and softly caressed my skin. My shoes were cotton with thin rubber soles. It was almost like I wasn't wearing anything at all. I needed to talk to Darlene about making sure these clothes were always available when I hunted.

The only pocket in my pants, by my right hip, contained my driver's license. I have never had a driver's license before. There wasn't a need for me to get one since I had never driven a car. Police never really bothered with me before. I don't think they never really noticed me, unless they happened to be a Were. Then like recognized like and they would just give me a sign of recognition and pass me by. This license wasn't even real. Father had handed me the card before we left our home. It had my picture on it, but it also added three years to my life giving my age as twenty-two. It also stated my name as Maria Christine Welhiem. The name fit me just as well as my legal name. I had no connection with my family so carrying another name didn't really bother me. I didn't think I would really need the card in the first place, but father explained many of the places he planned to take me to were operated by Were-creatures and they liked to make a big show about fitting in to the human society. This meant they would be looking for identification from anybody who tried to walk in their doors.

I wasn't really paying attention to where father was leading me, so I didn't know which casino we entered when he led me inside. The symphony of music coming from slot machines assaulted my ears. Machines pumped out music intermingled with the sounds of the dropping clang of coins. There was no evidence of coins dropping into bins beneath any machines I could see. Father led me down carpeted steps to the heart of the room. Gaming tables swarmed with patrons fingering multicolored chips and watching cards slide across the table. I recognized some of the games. One of the favorite activities of the asylum patrons were games of chance. As I watched the games being played my mind flashed on memories of games played by victims of my past. I could feel the exhilaration of the players shoot through my heart as I recalled memories that weren't mine.

Shaking my head, I cleared my mind of the invasive memories. I was standing close to father, trying to read his energy. He stood at ease in the middle of the chaos, smiling at all who met his eye. And there were several people smiling at father in return. It took a great deal of effort to push past the noise around me to find the energy I was searching for. I was surrounded by Were. Their energy was muted by the noise and lights all around us, but the markings were unmistakable. For every twenty human energy profile I read I saw at least one Were.

I was standing close to father and it seemed natural to place my hand in the bend of his elbow. He reached over and patted my hand with his own and led me deeper into the room. Flickers of energy danced around the room as we moved through the crowd. The humans bled their life force as their attention was caught up in the games of chance. Lights from the human energy danced around the room to be lapped up by the hovering Were.

We approached one of the half-moon shaped blackjack tables and my eyes were drawn to the flip of the cards. I watched as the cards fell in order in front of the players. Within seconds I added the numbers up and calculated the chances of each hand winning or losing. It was a game I played when old Charlie used to deal out cards at one of the rec rooms tables at the asylum. It was a little more difficult trying to figure out this game since it looked like the long, narrow rack holding the cards held several decks. Suddenly I understood the thrill of the flip of the cards, wondering if my calculations were correct and if the fall of the cards would mean winning or losing. Whether or not I gambled with money didn't really matter. If I ever needed money I took it off the bodies of my prey. I didn't need money very often. It wasn't high on my list of concerns.

We watched for a few more minutes and then father led me away from the tables and deeper into the room. Banks of slot machines continued to play their symphony of music as we walked by. Humans sat at the machines, staring like trapped creatures standing in bright lights as reels spun at great speeds. Energy seeped from the human forms huddled over the apparatuses sucking money into their inner reaches and giving out lights and music in return. The Were moved around the room drawing the escaping energy into their own bodies.

I noticed very few of the Were surrounding the humans spent any time at the gambling stations. They dealt cards or served drinks or wandered around the crowds performing services and being so inconspicuous they were completely unnoticed by the huddled masses. They fed freely, absorbing the energy bled by the humans. There was enough energy floating through the room for the Were to feast without needing to hunt for prey elsewhere. The humans probably didn't even realize their energy was being sapped away. Any ill effects they felt from the feedings would probably be dismissed as exhaustion, or drunkenness, or the flu. Some of the Were seemed strong enough to sap enough energy to cause severe illness in the humans, but none of them could even come close to draining the entire life-force from their prey. I began to realize just how truly unique I was.

If I was the only Were in the room then there might be enough latent energy to sustain me, for a while. I wanted to study my fellow creatures as they mingled through the crowd, but it was obvious father had other plans. He led me across the room to a Were standing behind an old man as he prodded the lit buttons of the slot machine. The man's hand shook as he reached for the spin button on the machine. I could see blue veins bulging from the translucent skin as he poked at the device.

As we approached the Were I could see her hand was not on the old man, but on an equally old woman seated at the slot machine next to him. The Were was drawing the energy from the woman slowly, so slowly the woman didn't even seem to be aware of the drain on her soul. I studied the Were as she stood behind the couple drawing on their energy. When the old man reached to place more money in the bill feeder of the machine the Were reached over and placed her hand over his to guide it to the slot. To all intents and purposes, it appeared she was helping steady his hand so he could slide the bill in with more ease, but I could see the drain of energy as she touched her hand to his.

The Were was dressed in attire suited more for a hospital worker than a casino worker. I recalled the propensity for the Were in Portland to work in the medical field to have easy access to prey and realized this was not an isolated phenomenon. Many Were must have discovered the availability of ready prey by those weakened by illness or injury.

Father approached the Were, leading me directly to her. I could see the mark of the family in her energy. She smiled at father as we came closer. Stepping away from her prey, she moved towards us and extended her arms to embrace father. I released his arm as he pulled her close, kissing her cheek.

"You are much stronger than the last time I saw you, child," he said. "I'm glad to see you are recovering."

I studied the woman, looking for signs of illness or injury. She looked strong, even though she was barely as big as me. Her body was slim and wiry with clearly defined muscles and her skin, although pale, glowed with energy. Wide, dark eyes shone brightly out of an oval face and short, dark hair curled around her head. The best description I could think of was pretty. She wasn't as pretty as Helena and Cassandra, but she was definitely prettier than me.

Father took me by the hand and pulled me forward. "Maria, this is your sister, Anna."

Her smile was warm and genuine as she opened her arms in a welcoming embrace. Another sister. I wondered just exactly how big this family was. I allowed her to embrace me, briefly. As I stepped back I glanced around, trying to read the other Were standing close by. They each had the markings of the Welhiem clan flowing within their energy. In just a few days I had gone from being a lone Were living on the streets to a member of an extensive family and living in a home grander than I could ever had imagined.

"How much longer will you care for your source?" Father asked, gesturing to the old couple still sitting at the machines. The old man looked like he had nodded off, his hand still hovering over the spin button. His wife was staring at the spinning reels, her face only inches from the screen and her rheumy blue eyes twitching without blinking.

Anna looked at the couple, her lips barely twitching to a weak smile. "It is getting close to the end," she said. "They are holding on to the last vestiges of their energy like a dog with a bone. I think I have taken all I can from them. After I put them to bed tonight I will be returning to the agency for a new assignment."

She turned back to her charges, a satisfied smile on her face. Father gently touched my elbow and guided me to the side of the room. He wrapped his arm around me and pulled me close.

"We will feed on those two tonight," he whispered. "This will satisfy our hunger and release Anna from her responsibilities here."

Anna was maneuvering a wheelchair to where the old man was sitting. I watched as she helped the man struggle into the contraption and positioned him for transport. The old woman pushed herself away from her machine and, retrieving her silver walker, toddled after her husband and the Were pushing him to the feast.

Chapter Twenty-Five

FATHER AND I WAITED near the elevator in the long, darkened hallway. We had spent nearly half an hour on the gaming floor waiting for Anna to prepare her charges for bed. Father led me to one of the machines and handed me a twenty-dollar bill.

"Here, play for a little while," he said. "Feel the energy of the machine. We sometimes like the distraction these devices give us."

I slid the bill into the machine. As soon as it disappeared lights flashed and the contraption started singing. Father was standing just over my shoulder. "If you read the energy right you can make it pay for you," he whispered.

The electricity of the machine buzzed and snapped as I slid my mind into the depths of the device. Energy crackled against my fingers as I reached for the spin-button. I sensed the pattern in the machine and twisted the energy as I pushed the button. The machine lit up and flashed as bells chimed. When the spinning stopped a line of bright red cherries glowed in each square across the center row of the machine. The numbers in the lower right corner started jumping as the machine paid off the jackpot. Father put his arm around me and whispered into my ear.

"I will have one of my children collect your winnings." He motioned for a nearby Were to approach. She was tiny and dark, like me, but she looked decades older. Father made a small gesture and I felt a buzz of energy spin around me and scatter across the room. I tucked my body closer to father as we moved away from the machine and towards the back of the building. A crowd had already started to gather from the area we had just abandoned, cheering as the machine continues to chime the sound of falling coins. "Well done, child. You just won yourself enough money to support yourself through several lifetimes, if you manage it carefully."

I shrugged my shoulders. "Why would I need money, father." I asked. "I don't live like the humans. All I need is shelter and food. All money can do is get me stuff. I'm not much of a collector of stuff. It's a human trait."

Father wrapped his arm around my shoulder and pulled me close. He led me to a bank of elevators, far away from any of the Were wandering around the casino floor. "Some of us are closer to being human than we are Were," he said. "We like stuff." I could hear the laughter in his voice as he said the word. "It makes our lives comfortable. Perhaps if we had more Were-spirit in us we wouldn't feel the need to have so much stuff."

As long as I had shelter over my head, food in my stomach and prey to hunt I had everything I needed to survive. Most of the time I didn't even need shelter since I rarely felt the effects of weather unless it was extreme. I wasn't very fond of cold, but I could survive a little wind, rain and sometimes snow.

As I watched the crowd around the machine grow I studied the woman who had replaced me at the controls. She seemed to be demonstrating the appropriate amount of excitement, embracing the patrons surrounding her and jumping up and down as she pointed at the machine. With every touch she drew off a little energy from the crowd surrounding her. Her aura brightened as the humans slowly bled off bits of themselves and she took it in, lapping up the energy like a bee syphoning nectar from brightly growing flowers. I looked around, trying to spy the surveillance cameras I knew were omnipresent in casinos, wondering if they would catch the switch father and I played on them. I glanced back at the woman, but I could barely see her through the crowd.

Father directed me to the bank of elevators at the back of the room. When an elevator door slid open we stepped inside. A man moved to enter with us, but father frowned and glared and the man stepped back, fear in his eyes, as he turned and sped away. The door slid shut and father pushed the button for the twenty-fourth floor. He touched the wall of the cart sending a burst of energy from his hand into the electrical system. I heard a popping sound and could smell the scent of burning wires.

"That takes care of the cameras in here." Father turned and grinned at me. "I'm quite impressed, child. There are only a few of us capable of manipulating the machines. I wouldn't recommend doing it very often, at least not until you develop your own team. It's easy to make money here, but you need to keep a low profile and winning multiple jackpots tends to bring attention you may not want."

The last thing I wanted was attention. I knew that much at least. "Won't they know we switched with the other woman?" I asked.

"You're not the only one who can manipulate energy and create illusions," Father explained. "I made sure the cameras didn't see the switch. No one will know the difference when they pay Katherine the money and she will bring it to you."

I shrugged, turning and facing the metal doors of the elevator. "She can keep the money."

Father patted my shoulder as the elevator doors slid open. "You may want it someday, child. It makes living among our prey very pleasant at times."

The doors slid open and father and I slipped into the long, narrow hallway. Sconces glowed dimly from the recesses high on the walls and orange-brown carpet seemed to drown the hall in drab loneliness. Father looked up at the ceiling and smiled. The lights flickered and buzzed as energy surged along the corridor.

"That'll take care of the cameras," father said. "No one will see us."

I followed him down the hall counting the room numbers as we passed each door. We were nearly at the end of the hall when father turned and gently tapped on a door. We were only two doors down from the exit leading to the stairs. The door swung open and Anna gestured for us to enter. She smiled as I walked by her and entered the room.

"They're ready for you father," she said. "She has more energy than he does, but they are both close to the end."

I glanced around the room. Two double beds dominated the space in the sparsely furnished room. The square footage didn't allow for much more than the beds and a dresser with a flat screen television. The beds were empty and completely undisturbed, as if they hadn't been slept in at all. There was no one else in the room.

Father followed Anna past the bathroom to a door tucked on the far wall. She opened the door and stood aside, allowing a full view of the room beyond.

This room was large in comparison to the one we were standing in, however it only had one bed. The occupants of the bed were lying flat on their backs, mouths gaping open as they sucked oxygen into their lungs with rattling breaths. I recognized the woman from the slot machines first. The man's skin loosely sloped away from his face forcing his nose and cheekbones to stand in sharp relief. His lips were tainted blue and fell concave into his toothless mouth.

Anna turned to father's embrace. He held her close for a moment. I could see the energy exchange between the two as her energy melted into father's and he strengthened her with threads of his own. When she stepped out of his embrace he kept his hands on her shoulders and looked deep into her eyes. "I'm glad you were able to recover from Sebastian's attack," he said.

Anna's body was trembling, but she had a shy smile on her face as she responded to father's caring gestures. "He's trying to eat away at the edges of our coven, father," she said. "I'm afraid for you. He's getting stronger and it won't be long before he attacks you directly."

Father shook his head. "He's too much of a coward to attack me directly. He'll keep hitting us at the edges until he is too weak or until I gather our forces to confront him. He's no more than a mosquito buzzing around my head. I'll swat him down, eventually."

He released Anna's shoulders and directed her to one of the beds. "You know the routine," he said. "When you do your next two hour rounds you will find the woman dead and the old man barely alive. Contact the doctor in charge. He will take care of the bodies. Now, go get some rest."

Father gestured for me to follow him into the next room. I trailed after him, eyeing the couple as their rasping snores filled the room. Neither of them woke as we leaned over their bodies. Father beside him, me beside his wife. Her breath was warm in my nostrils and I drew in the scent of her, filling my own lungs with the sweetness of her energy. I leaned to drink my fill when her eyes suddenly flew open. Light blue eyes wavered just centimeters from mine. I saw them flood with fear and a gasp escaped her lips. Clamping my own mouth over hers, I swallowed her scream with her energy. Her weak struggles soon ceased as she released the tiny fragments of her soul to me.

She didn't have much to give, but it was enough to give me strength and sustain me for a while. The energy buzzed around my head blurring the edges of my vision. I grabbed the edges of the bed, keeping my body upright while I adjusted to her mind. She was very old and had lived a long, fulfilling life. Her pain was vague, mostly centered on physical ailments. I tasted the sweetness of her life as it scattered through my body.

My legs were quivering. I didn't have much time. Pushing myself away from the bed, I staggered to the doorway. Grasping the edges of the doorframe, I attempted to keep to my feet, but it was no use. My knees gave way and I tumbled to the floor. Father's arms encircled me, lifting me from the carpet and carrying me to the bed.

"Don't try to keep the energy in your head, child." His mouth was right against my ear as he whispered the words. "Bring it down to your core."

I tried to obey. My head was so full I could feel myself spinning out of control. Her memories bounced around my head. Mostly they centered around her daughter and son and their children. I kept seeing them run and play. And the laughter, oh, it just spun in my head, turning over and over, spinning until I was dizzy. Closing my eyes, I let the blackness take over.

When I woke I was no longer in the hotel room. Father must have carried me away from there like he had the alley. Blinking, I cleared away the remnants of the shadows from my mind. I expected to be in my room, but the light was too bright. My body was being supported by soft cushions. Once my head cleared I realized I was lying on the couch in the living room of father's home.

I sat up, looking around for the others. No one else was in the room. Reaching out with my mind, I searched for their energies. Darlene was somewhere outside. I could feel her satisfaction as she scraped and dug in the soil. The others were scattered throughout the house. I could feel their energy surge and pulse with their actions.

Slowly pulling myself from the couch, I walked towards the back of the house. I was steps away from the weapons' room when Cassandra appeared in the doorway. She reached out and grabbed my hand, pulling me the rest of the way into the room.

"Come on," she said, "let's play."

The skirt of her red dress flared as she spun to the center of the room. When she stopped she raised her arm level to the ground. A beam from the setting sun flashed through the window and glinted off the point of a very sharp looking foil. A slow smile spread across her face, revealing bright, white teeth.

"Come on, sister. I won't make you bleed, much." She pushed the tip of her tongue through her teeth as her grin widened.

Chapter Twenty-Six

I TOOK A BACKWARDS step towards the door and nearly ran into Stephen as he entered the room. Cassandra winked and gestured with her sword for him to approach. He shook his head once and then motioned towards the door at the back of the room.

"Are Helena and father out there?" he asked.

"They're playing in the rock garden." Cassandra said. Her mouth was turned down in a pout and her voice sounded like it was buried deep in her nasal passages. "No one wants to play with me." Suddenly she grinned and her voice become cajoling. "Do you want to play with me Stephen?" she asked. "I might even let you win this time."

Stephen looked at me and then looked at Cassandra. He shook his head but moved to the wall and picked up a foil.

"You shouldn't tease our new sister so much," he said. "We don't want to scare her away."

I smiled as Stephen took up a defensive position a few feet in front of Cassandra. Sunlight filtered through the window, flashing off the tip of his foil. This was no blunt ended sparing tool. I could see the sharp definition of the tip of the sword as he lunged.

They blurred into action. A bright spinning of light and movement. Cassandra's dress floated around her as she spun, filling the room with bright flashes of red silk. Stephen was a blur of black and white as he flipped and spun, countering Cassandra's thrusts. I'm not sure who drew first blood, but when they were finished they both stood facing each other, blood oozing from beneath shredded clothing.

Stephen removed his shirt and used it to wipe the blood from his torso. The wounds were already sealed, leaving barely visible red marks beneath the smeared blood. Even as I watched the red marks began to fade away. Blood still oozed from slash marks on Cassandra's arms and chest. A deep welt on her right wrist dripped with bright red blood. Cassandra raised her arm and licked the blood as it dripped down her fingers. The crimson fluid stained her lips and smeared across her chin. Pressing her wrist against her lips, she drank the blood from her wound.

"Cassandra, stop!"

Father's voice brought us all up short. He was entering the room from the rock garden. Helena entered right behind him and approached her daughter. With a swift motion she pulled Cassandra's arm away from her mouth. Cassandra snarled, showing blood-stained teeth. The slap was so fast I heard it more than saw it as Helena brought her hand across her daughter's face.

Cassandra crumpled to the floor clutching her cheek. Tears sparkled in her eyes but they didn't fall. Her mother raised her hand again but father moved forward and restrained her before the blow could fall.

"That's enough Helena." He said. His voice was soft as he helped Cassandra up off the floor. "Take her and give her a shower. The bleeding has already stopped. Once she has been cleansed she will have no more to drink."

Helena led her daughter out of the room. Stephen picked up the foil Cassandra had abandoned, bringing the weapon to a table set up in the corner of the room. He used a cloth to clean the blades.

"Stephen," father said. "You know she isn't going to be satisfied with a little taste of blood."

Stephen didn't turn to face father, but he did acknowledge the words with a barely perceptible nod.

"You will take her out hunting tonight." Father's words were gentle, but I heard the note of command in his voice. "Go to Wyland's territory. There is an increase in the fighting between the two gangs trying to control his streets. No one will notice another stabbing victim in the melee. Wyland will be able to direct you to some likely sources. He keeps a pretty tight grip on the humans in his hunting grounds."

I watched as Stephen replaced the foils into the rack on the wall. After he was finished he turned towards the door. He didn't even glance in father's direction.

"Stephen, look at me," father commanded.

I could almost sense the hesitation in Stephen's body as he turned around and faced father. He kept his eyes downcast as father spoke to him.

"I'm not angry, son." Father said. "Cassandra can be very persistent when she wants to play. I'm sure her appetite will be satisfied when she feeds tonight. I would take her if we didn't have our newest member of the family to take care of."

Stephen lifted his eyes, glancing at me before looking at father.

"I shouldn't have let her entice me into playing." Stephen said. "I've just been so restless lately and I wanted to take it out on someone. Cassie likes to play rough."

Father crossed the room to Stephen and embraced him. "I am glad you are recovering your strength and willingness to fight. We are all going to need to be at full strength when we confront Sebastian."

Stephen returned father's embrace before turning towards the door. His mannerism had changed and I detected a smile creeping around his lips as he passed me. I couldn't help but return his smile. Father was inspecting the weapons displayed in the racks mounted on the wall. He reached up and removed a short sword from the center of one rack.

"Would you like to start with sword work?" He asked.

He must have sensed my confusion because he placed the sword on the table and walked across the room to confront me.

"Why are you afraid, child?" He asked. "I'm not going to hurt you. I just want to teach you how to fight."

I chewed on my bottom lip, trying to frame my answer. Learning to fight with weapons really didn't make sense to me. I had never confronted an enemy I didn't know how to defeat.

"I'm not afraid, father," I said. "I just don't understand why I need to learn to use weapons. My prey falls easily into my hands. None of them have the strength to defeat me."

Father smiled and placed his hand on my shoulder. "We don't need to use weapons on our prey, Maria," he said. "The humans are inconsequential to us. They are merely a source for sustenance. We learn to use these weapons so we are prepared for war with others of our kind."

I reflected on the fight I had with Sebastian and the others in his coven. Studying the wall of weapons in front of me, I considered how the battle would have ended if I had a sword in my hand. I knew I could have easily defeated Sebastian without the aid of any weapon. He would have been badly injured, but he could have easily recovered. Perhaps he would figure out I wasn't someone he could easily intimidate and would leave me alone. None of the others of my kind bothered me when I lived in Portland.

"How bad is the war between our kinds here?" I asked. "We didn't fight bloody battles in the streets of Portland."

"Are you sure about that?" Father raised his eyebrow, giving a sardonic twist to his face as he asked the question. "Why are you here, child? You're running away from something."

The memory of clear eyes glowing from black-dark skin raised the hackles on the back of my neck. I pushed down the memory of the death of the Were in the graveyard and returned my attention to father.

"I wasn't running from other Were," I said. "I was running from a creature who killed Were. I've never seen anyone like him before."

"Yes," father said. "I remember seeing him in your memories. The Warrior is a special race of creatures. They are as powerful and long-lived as the Were, but there aren't as many of them as there are of us. Just as there are only a few powerful Were born in each generation, there are only a few Warriors born within their tribes. And they can also be killed in much the same way we can kill other Were."

I nodded my understanding. If there were only a few Warriors in the world it would be an easy thing to avoid them.

"Why do I need to learn to fight Were?" I asked. "I have no quarrel with other Were. All I'm interested in is my own survival."

Father shook his head and placed his arm around my shoulder. "You don't have that option any more, Maria," he said. "You're a part of my coven now and you need to help us defend our territory. Your grandfather would expect the same if you stayed in the Pacific Northwest territories."

"I don't understand. My grandfather didn't have to defend his territory," I said. "Were didn't fight each other. Why do we need to kill other Were? Isn't there enough prey for all of us to feed?"

"We don't battle for prey, child," father replied. "We battle for territory and for family. As long as humans keep breeding we will have unlimited resource for prey. We need to protect our hunting grounds. Your grandfather fights this battle just as we do. It's why he brought his daughter the witch to feed upon. He was trying to make her strong enough to take on my sister."

I had personally felt Agnes' strength when she tried to take possession of my body. She was almost stronger than I was. From the few flashes I remembered of my mother I knew she was strong, but not nearly as strong as me.

"How am I going to fight and still be able to hunt?" I have never gone more than three days without hunting. Without feeding my energy reserves would easily wane and I would start losing strength.

Giving my shoulder a squeeze, father released me and headed back to the wall of weapons. I followed him, realizing I was becoming excited about the prospect of fighting with these bright, shining implements.

Father took down the same slim sword he held out to me before, handing it to me hilt first. "You will find you won't need to hunt as often as you learn to store and control your energy consumption," he explained. "And we don't really battle very often. Every once in a while, some coven will decide to challenge another. Sebastian was once a member of this coven. He was a much my son as you are my daughter, but he decided to strike out on his own." I could see the sorrow in father's eyes as he talked about his wayward son. "We didn't begrudge his defection, but he wanted to gouge his territory from our own. He killed and injured many of our members in his quest for territory. Right now, he is biding his time, but I know he will try to strike at us again and we all need to be prepared," he said. "And you'll be surprised by how much strength you will gain from feasting on Were-energy."

I took the sword and let the hilt settle into my grasp. Waving it back and forth, I judged its balance. The weight of the blade dragged at my wrist and the blade dipped towards the ground more often than I liked.

"Don't worry child," father said. "You'll learn how to use these weapons soon. It's not difficult."

I wrapped my other hand around the hilt to steady the blade. Light filtering in through the window caught the tip causing it to flash with a brilliant glow. A slow smile crept up my face as the warmth of the light filled my chest. Father's face lit up in a matching smile as he too took a sword from the wall.

"I've never feasted on the energy of another Were before," I said. "My mother feasted on a witch. That's what caused her to go insane."

Father shook his head and pointed his sword to the ground. "Your mother went insane because she wasn't prepared for your awakening powers. It had nothing to do with feasting on a witch," he said. "Witches draw their power from the energy of the earth. Their energy is much closer to humans than Were. They are lesser creatures, just like humans. Darlene is fairly powerful, despite her limited abilities. I think your powers would have been awoken no matter what kind of creature your mother feasted upon. You are truly unique, child."

He raised his sword again. This time I lifted my sword in response. I could feel the hilt settle in my palm as if it was an extension of my arm. Images of what my responses should be flashed through my mind. I recognized some of them as coming from a few of my former victims, but some of them were vague recollections planted in my head from the bonding I shared with father and the other members of my coven. Sunlight flashed off my blade as I brought it up against father's.

Chapter Twenty-seven

I SHOOK THE RAIN from my hair and wiped the back of my hand across my face. The roof of the apartment complex was dark, hiding me from prying eyes, but there was no shelter from the rain dumping from the overcast clouds. I wondered if we should head down to the Strip. The heat reflecting from the pavement and lights of the boulevard evaporated the rain before it could strike the ground. We would still be damp from the high humidity, but we wouldn't be drenched. Stephen and Cassandra were somewhere behind me on another rooftop. They were searching for their own prey. Cassandra was giddy and her chatter had been getting on my nerves. It was difficult getting used to hunting with the others, but with the growing threat of Sebastian and his followers it wasn't safe to hunt alone.

I thought about striking out on my own but leaving the others would mean disappointing father. It amazed me that in just a few short months pleasing father had become central to my existence. He wasn't difficult to please. My progress with weapons work alone was enough to make him smile and heap praise upon me.

Adjusting the strap carrying my short sword across my back, I reached for the hilt. The silver pommel and sheath were covered by a weather guard, protecting it from the rain, but I could easily release the sword and draw it if I needed it. There hadn't been a need for me to use my weapon, yet, but I always carried one on me just in case.

There was any number of weapons I could have learned from the wall in the training room, but father had limited me to swords and long knives since I joined the coven. I had mentioned my desire to learn how to use a bow and arrow, admiring a highly polished, black bow he had placed on the wall only a few weeks ago. Father just shook his head and placed a sword in my hand.

"You'll have millennia to study bow work and other such weaponry, child," he explained. "They're such crude weapons anyway. When you shoot a Were from a distance you don't have time to draw in his energy before he either heals or dies. It's a waste of energy to even try. The only time we use these weapons is when their force is more powerful than ours and we need to attack from concealed locations. Sebastian is nowhere near strong enough to overpower our coven. You'll do well enough with a sword in your hands."

Training hardly interrupted my hunting and my newly learned focus allowed me to go much longer between feedings. Although I still syphoned energy off many creatures through latent feedings on nearly a daily basis, I could go a full week without needing to completely drain my prey. The others didn't need to feed as often as I did, but one or two of them always accompanied me on my outings.

Stephen was my most frequent companion. He was an easy ally, not needing to fill in uncomfortable silences with unnecessary conversations. I would hunt, Stephen would watch my back and then we would go home. Sometimes father would send us on a task, deliver a message to a member of the coven, scout the edges of our territory, or seek out other coven leaders to see if they've had incursions into their territory.

Father was teaching me more about the power of my mind as he taught me about weaponry. There were elements to my powers I still had yet to explore. Agnes had taught me how to use my physical strength, but I had no idea there was so much power yet to explore in my mind. Even now I reached out to Stephen and Cassie and allowed them to see what I was seeing.

Everything was still and quiet. The rain had slowed to little more than a drizzle and I could hear the city coming back as the gentle hiss of rain slowly faded. Between the height of the building and its distance from the Strip, I was far enough from the bright lights of the city I had a clear view of the sky. The clouds were beginning to part and I caught a glimpse of stars twinkling through the gaps. Turning my face to the clouds I drank in the rain and the stars and the moment. For just that second, I felt like I was home.

I hadn't realized how much I missed the streets of Portland until just this moment. It was always wet in the city, but the greenery surrounding the buildings and sprouting above the streets kept me dry enough. I was lonely for the streets and alleys I knew so well. I was learning the streets here but getting used to new hunting grounds was taking time. By this point in my hunt I would have found my victim, fed and been curled up in some hole waiting out the after effects.

I felt rather than heard the thud of Cassie's and Stephen's shoes on the roof behind me. I waited until they caught up to me before swinging down the side of the building and scaling the forty stories to the ground. Cassie and Stephen leapt from window ledge to window ledge, clinging to the two-inch protrusions with as much concern as they would have if the space was a meter wide. They both touched down on the ground before I did, but just barely.

"There's nothing here," Stephen said. "They've all skittered inside to get out of the rain."

"Maybe they'll come out now that the rain is stopping." I looked up and down the street, looking for any sign of movement from darkened doorways and alleys.

Stephen grabbed Cassie's hand and started pulling her along with him. "Nay," he said. "In this kind of weather, the rabbits hole up. Once they're in for the night they usually stay in."

I followed him as he led us down through the streets and closer to the Strip. We moved fast, because we could. There's a certain magic to our movement. Stephen and Cassandra seemed to glide, barely touching the ground as light surrounded them. I followed, my footsteps silent as I ran as fast as them, albeit with less grace. We didn't go as far as the Strip. There really wasn't a need to. Stephen led us to a dingy street just about a mile from the main drag. Away from the lights of the Strip the buildings looked dull and lifeless. Dark figures danced in and out of the shadows of buildings and the air buzzed with energy. Opening my mouth slightly, I allowed myself to taste the essence. It danced across my tongue and made my cheeks tingle.

The streets were still wet and the pavement sparkled as it refracted the light from the gas station on the corner. I could see a few businesses, a pawn shop, a bar and what looked like a tattoo parlor nestled in the shadow of a brightly light casino. The bright lights of the gas station and casino just made everything else look dim and dirty. Stephen led us down the block, past small groups of people, each intent on their own goals. I eyed a group of three men staggering from the bar and heading towards a row of cars nearly obscured in a tiny parking lot. They were drunk enough we could overpower them. By the time we were finished with them they would look like victims of a mugging or casualties of a bar fight. It wouldn't be the first time we used this ruse to cover our tracks. Stephen and Cassie could even have their own source, although they wouldn't be able to drain them completely. I would have to finish them off or we would have to kill them with one of the weapons we carried with us. I started gathering my energy around myself, sending my intentions to the others.

Stephen tapped my shoulder and shook his head. He gestured to something across the street. It took me a moment to read his intentions, but movement in the darkness drew my attention to the figures just ducking into the shadow between two buildings. I opened my mouth a little more and tasted the tingle of their energy. My cheeks tightened as the energy burned my senses. It was different. More subtle. Softer. A scent I was just beginning to recognize.

We followed Stephen across the street and into the shadows. It took me a moment to find the forms in the darkness. The sounds of grunts and groans filled the emptiness. I realized I couldn't make out the two forms because the individuals were intertwined. The male had the female pinned against the wall, his pants down around his ankles.

"Stop messing around and give me what I paid for." The man's voice was husky as he nearly growled out the words.

The woman wasn't acting like a person in the throes of passion. Her hands pressed against the man's forearms and her face was turned away from his. He didn't seem to notice her apparent aversion to his actions, intent only on his own satisfaction.

Sliding her hands up the man's arms, the woman buried her fingers into his hair. She twisted strands of his hair into her grasp and jerked his head back. A strangled cry escaped his lips as she brought her mouth to his throat. I recognized the gesture. I used it often enough myself.

Before her lips descended to the pulse point at her prey's neck Cassandra made her move. In less than a second the man was huddled on the opposite wall and Cassandra had taken his place, forcing the other woman against the wall with her own body. Drawing her sword, she pressed the point of the blade against the woman's ribcage and slid it into her body. The woman gurgled, but she stayed upright. The injury was just enough to disable her, but it wasn't life-threatening. I moved with Stephen to the form of the man. He seemed so much smaller separated from the woman and huddled on the ground, his skin quivered as he shook in his fear. His pants were still drooping around his ankles, exposing a broad expanse of pale, white flesh.

Stephen reached the man and lifted him from the ground. He twisted him until they were both facing me. The man dangled from Stephen's arms, his scrawny legs kicked in a futile attempt at escape. I looked from Stephen's victim to Cassie's, wondering which one I should take. Cassie and Stephen would share the one I didn't choose. I took a step towards Stephen and the man, but he shook his head and nodded toward Cassandra. As I turned toward my sister, I realized she was struggling with the woman. Leaping across the space between us, I grabbed the woman and dragged her to the ground. She twisted and turned in my grasp, slithering as I pinned her and pulled her arms over her head.

"He's mine!" she growled. Her body arched as she tried to buck me off.

Stephen and Cassie had already exposed the neck of the man and started to feed. I could sense their satisfaction as the man's energy slowly drained from his body. Lowering my face to the woman's, I placed my mouth over hers.

Chapter Twenty-eight

SHE WAS SO SWEET. It was almost as if I was drinking honey through a straw. I slowly drew her life-force from her body, savoring the taste and bringing it to my core. Her struggles continued, but I could begin to feel her weaken as I stole her energy from her core.

I could feel the rising energy fill my body starting at the bottom of my feet and working its way to the top of my head. This wasn't like any feeding I had ever done before. It was filling my body with white-hot electric pulses. I slowed down, allowing the sensation to envelop me.

She finally stopped struggling. Her breath came in short, labored gasps as I drew in even more of her energy. I sensed the others behind me, positioning the body of their victim to make it look like he had been jumped and beaten by thieves. It was a common enough ruse. The marks left by our feedings looked similar to bruises and Cassandra always seemed to leave extra marks when she fed. Bruises and slashes marking her corpses gave testament to the violence of her feedings.

I was nearly finished with mine when I felt Stephen reach into my mind. Lifting my mouth off my prey I looked to see what he wanted. He knelt beside me and touched the woman's face. She whimpered as his fingers slid down her cheek and settled around her neck.

"What are you doing hunting in our territory?" he asked.

The woman moaned and tried to pull away from him. He flexed his fingers and her face started to change to a bright red as she gasped for air. Arching her back, she managed to free one of her hands and claw at Stephen. Her fingernails left bloody marks on the back of his hands. I recaptured her hand and pinned it under my knee. She moaned as the bones crunched, snapping like dry twigs.

"Answer me!" Stephen's face was inches from hers as he growled out the words.

"Sebastian!" Her words came out in a strangled cry. Stephen released the pressure on her throat but didn't remove his hand. "He told us we needed to expand our territory. He wants us to find new hunting grounds. I'm just doing what he told me to do."

Stephen released her throat but brought his face even closer to hers. "Are you linked to him?" She closed her eyes, nodding her answer. "Let him know we are aware of his attempts to steal into our territory. We have cast our nets wide and we will catch any of his coven trying to sneak into our hunting grounds."

Her face was pale and her red-rimmed eyes were opened so wide I could see every blood vessel in the whites of her eyes. Despite the darkness, her pupils were pinpoints of black in her bright, blue irises. "I'll tell him." The words were whispered, but I could hear the catch in her throat as she swallowed back a sob.

"Tell him now!" Stephen growled the words. Her whole body quivered as she closed her eyes. I could feel the whisper of her thought as she sent it to her coven leader. "Did he hear you?" Stephen asked. She nodded. Stephen moved back and I swooped in, covering her mouth with mine. It only took mere seconds to drain the last of her energy.

Her body crumpled in on itself, collapsing under me. I pushed myself off the ground and watched as her body transformed into particles of dust. A slight breeze stirred the remains, but the humidity was so high the ashes didn't move very far. I knew the signs of my victim would be obliterated by the time the sun rose in the morning, but we still needed to be far away from the body of the man before the curious found him.

Working our way around the dark side of the building, we moved back out on to the street and headed towards home. Cassie led the way and Stephen walked beside me, staying close as we slipped through the shadows. Since father started teaching me to control the energy I consumed I rarely succumbed to my seizures, but someone always stood beside me in case I fell.

It was still hours before sunrise when we made our way home. I could feel my feet dragging as we walked up the sidewalk and approached the front door. My body buzzed with the newly consumed energy and the thought of entering the stifling confines of a house, even one as spacious as ours, seemed to oppress me.

Cassie sensed my hesitation and turned back to us. Grasping my hand, she pulled me towards the door. "Don't worry, sis," she said. "We don't need to stay inside. Father will want to hear about our hunt, then we can go play in the rock garden."

I couldn't help but smile at Cassie's enthusiasm. She could be quite charming when she was at her most playful. It was easy to see past the quirks of her appetites. In the end it didn't really matter how our prey died. My own aversion to the taste of blood didn't prevent me from feeding as efficiently as she did. Just because she liked to drink the blood of her victims as she drained their energy didn't make her any more of a monster than it did me. Our victims ended up just as dead at the end of the feeding.

We breezed past Darlene as she opened the door for us. I could smell the food she prepared for us in the dining room, but I wasn't hungry. I knew the food would be there for us later, it always was. We only ate together as a family a few times a week. None of us ate very much, but it was nice knowing there was always plenty of food around.

Father met us in the training room and, sensing our mood, followed us outside. The rain had let up, but the air was still weighed down with humidity. A brightness in the east foreshadowed the rising of the sun. Morning was only a few minutes away. The wind shredded the remaining clouds, sending tattered puffs of white cloud across the horizon.

"Are you hurt?" Father asked. He was staring at my legs. Looking down, I realized my pants were covered with blood.

I shook my head. "It's not my blood." I explained. "Cassie injured a Were so I could feed. She was a member of Sebastian's coven hunting in our territory."

"Show me what happened." Father reached for me and I allowed him to draw me into his arms.

Father's embrace encompassed me, drawing me into the warmth of his energy. Leaning forward, I placed my forehead against his. It only took a few moments to share the experience with him, but I held our position for a few extra seconds, drawing on his strength.

"You are gaining new skills every day." I could hear the pleasure in his voice.

"I feel stronger than ever." I stepped back and stretched, allowing my muscles to stretch and fall into place. "I can still feel her bouncing around inside me. It's like she's trying to get out. I can control her, though. It won't take me long to incorporate her energy into mine. Is this what it'll be like every time?"

Father smiled and reached out to embrace me. I returned his embrace without any qualms, something I would have never done three months ago. "It's quite exhilarating. We don't feed on our own very often," he explained. "But I have a feeling you'll be getting the opportunity to feed on more before long. Sebastian's people are encroaching on our hunting grounds and we can't allow it."

"What happened to her body?" I asked. "Why did it crumble to dust?" It was a question I had been meaning to ask, but there was so much to learn I never really got around to it. I had theories about why it happened, but I wanted to know the reality behind the reasoning.

Father released me but kept his arm around my shoulders as we walked around the garden. The stench from the blood on my clothes was getting stronger and I realized I would need to go inside to change and shower before I meditated. I wouldn't be able to concentrate if I didn't.

"We are more energy than matter, I think," father explained. "Of course, not all energy beings dissolve into dust once their energy leaves their body. Those capable of shape-shifting seem to be the only ones who disintegrate in this manner. We are stronger than many of the others and tend to be better feeders as well. Witches decompose at the same rate as humans. They also don't live as long as we do."

"How long will I live?" I had never thought of my own mortality. I always assumed I would live out my life, grow old and die in the normal human lifespan. The more I learned about my abilities the more I realized I was something other than human.

"No one can measure the length of our lives," father replied. "I have lived over five thousand years. Helena was captured by the Greeks from her village in Italy many centuries ago. She was kept by the men in the army and used horribly. Cassandra was born as a result of her captivity. I believe it is why she despises her daughter so much. I have no way of knowing her true age because she refuses to speak to me about those events. She joined my coven and has been under my protection for the past two thousand years." Father stopped walking and studied the others as they danced and ran among the rocks. Cassandra was chasing Stephen in a complicated game of tag.

"Stephen was born three-hundred years ago," father continued in his explanation. "I have seen children born, grow to an old age and die all within my lifetime. Some only live the same amount of time as humans, some for hundreds, if not thousands of years. Our people don't have very many children throughout our lifetime and not every child born has the ability to feed and change shape. Our ability to draw in energy and use it to strengthen our own bodies seem to be tied directly to the length of our lives. I believe you are like me. If you learn to control your feeding and your energy consumption you can live in this form for thousands of years."

We were near the entrance of the training center. The smell of the blood on my clothing was becoming cloying and I knew I wouldn't be able to concentrate until I showered and changed. Father opened the door and gestured for me to enter.

"Go get cleaned up," he said. "There is much more to learn and I can sense your discomfort. We will talk after you meditate."

The smell of blood was overwhelming. I realized both my pants and shirt were stained with great red splotches. I knew I wasn't going to be able to meditate as long as the stench was clinging to me. With a sigh, I headed inside. Darlene was waiting for me when I entered my room. She took the clothes as I stripped them off and stuffed them into a paper bag. She would bring them to another coven member to be incinerated in the crematory he managed. We would sometimes bring the bodies of our victims to him for disposal. It was an effective method of hiding our tracks. The desert was another resource for disposal. Wind, sand, sun and carrion eaters worked well to hide the markings of our feedings.

I showered and changed into fresh clothing. The cotton shirt and leggings were my favorite, although father provided me with a wide variety of clothing options. He was spoiling me with food and clothing and shelter. And he was using his own money to do it. I had never felt so sheltered in my life. I left the bedroom, glancing at the bed I never used, and headed back outside. Cassie and Stephen were waiting for me in the shadow of my favorite tower.

Chapter Twenty-nine

FATHER WAS SOMEWHERE DEEP in the rock garden. I thought about seeking him out, but I needed to spend some time meditating. My head was buzzing with unused energy and I wanted to get it all sorted out before I played with the others. As soon as Cassie and Stephen saw me they headed to two of the tallest rocks in the garden and scrambled to the top. Facing each other at the top of their perch, they stretched their bodies and crouched low. Cassie pushed off first, but Stephen followed soon after. They made a running leap at each other, grabbed each other's forearms and twisted through the air. Using the momentum, they pushed away from each other and landed on a pair of rocks farther down the path. They would be at this game for hours. Twisting and turning and flying through the air. Any other time I would have joined them, but my need to meditate took precedence. Walking down the path to my favorite rock, I climbed to the top and settled in and allowed the morning sun to bask me with its rays.

By midmorning the sun had dried up the last of the moisture from the air. The desert heat was starting to reassert itself, kicking up bits of sand and dirt. I was high enough off the ground I barely felt the effects, but Stephen and Cassie wanted to go inside and practice with the swords. I wasn't quite ready to leave my warm spot so when they came to retrieve me I told Stephen I wanted to spend some more time meditating.

Closing my eyes, I absorbed the energy of the sun, allowing the rays to caress me and center my focus. I stretched out, allowing the warmth of the rock to penetrate my shoulder blades. The winds picked up bringing even more sand and grit with it. There was something else in the sound of the wind. A voice coming from somewhere around me.

I sat up and looked around, trying to see where the sound was coming from. It was hard to hear. I wasn't even sure if it was a voice the sound was so faint. Standing, I gazed at the area surrounding my rock. I was above the rooftops of the neighborhood and could see the reflections off many of the glass buildings deep in the city. Our back yard covered acres of land and was dotted with scrubby looking trees and great monoliths of rocks. Father had created the landscape many years ago, long before the city grew into the mecca it was today. He knew what the city would grow to become and knew it would be the perfect hunting ground for his coven.

There was no movement on the ground except for bits of sand being blown around by the wind. I tried to peer through the rocks and trees, but I couldn't detect anyone hiding in the shadows. I had just about convinced myself I was hearing things when the whisper called my name. I spun around and studied the edges of the grounds. A high rock wall encased the property, hiding it from prying eyes, but I still couldn't see anyone.

"Cassie!" I called my sister's name. It would be just like her to hide in the rock garden and try to surprise me. I heard her voice call to me from inside the training room.

The voice called my name again. This time I heard it distinctly. And I knew it wasn't Cassie. The voice calling for me was male. I crouched, preparing to spring at the threat, if he ever showed himself.

There was a shimmering of light at the opposite corner of my rock. A form was beginning to take shape. I held my crouch as the figure of a man began to coalesce across from me. My lips curled back into a snarl as I recognized him.

"So, this is where you've been hiding," he said.

"Leave me, priest," I spat out. "I will rip you to shreds."

The man had the audacity to laugh at me. "You don't scare me," he said. "What do you think you are any way?"

"I'm the monster under the bed. I'm the thing that goes bump in the night. You should be afraid of me." I shifted my feet, making sure I was perfectly balanced and ready to spring. He didn't move. He didn't even react to the deep, glottal growl behind my words.

I reached out for the others with my thoughts. My mind seemed to recoil on itself as I stretched to try to find them. There was a wall between me and my family. I could sense them, but I couldn't reach out to their minds and connect. Something was blocking me. I narrowed my eyes and studied the priest. He was standing at the edge of the rock a tight smile dancing around the corners of his mouth.

"I don't need the others to destroy you, priest." I growled at him.

A heavy weight settled on my shoulders, pinning me to the rock. I twisted my body, torqueing it until my bones creaked. The bond held me in place and I was unable to lift my feet and propel myself towards him. I could feel his restraining force like thick chains twining around me and shackling me to the basalt pillar.

"Release me!" The command carried all the weight I could muster, but I could feel the invisible chains binding me. I tried twisting my body, fighting against the pressure holding me to the rock.

He slowly inched towards me. As he approached I could feel the bonds tightening around my shoulders and chest. My breath came in short gasps and bright spots popped in front of my eyes. A low growl bubbled up in my throat but I couldn't get enough air to get any volume. The priest stalked me to the edge of the rock. It took everything in me to stay on my feet.

"I want you," his eyes pinned me in place. I couldn't look away.

I hissed as he reached for me. The sound must have startled him. His hands fell away and I could feel the bindings loosen. I still wasn't free. He had me tightly in his grip. Gasping, I continued to struggle, fighting against the weight he was piling on me.

"You will never take me." The words came out in a hoarse whisper. "I won't be forced. I will mate when I choose."

He stopped in his approach, a wide grin spread across his face. "I have no interest in mating with you." He placed his hands on either side of my head. "I want to be a part of you. There is so much power running through your body." He brought his face closer to mine and took a deep breath. "You smell so good."

He brought his lips closer to mine. The force of his energy tingled across my face.

"Let me go!" I growled at him.

He shook his head, his lips brushing against mine. "We belong to each other, creature," he whispered.

I couldn't struggle against him anymore. As he moved forward I allowed my muscles to go completely slack. His energy pushed against me, trying to force its way into my body.

My heels were at the edge of the rock. The flow of his energy pushed against me and as I relaxed my body I could feel myself falling. Reaching around, I wrapped my arms around his neck and pulled him towards the edge of the rock. We twisted in the air as the ground rushed up towards us. I made sure I was on top of him as we hit the ground.

The bonds fell away, releasing my body from its restrictions. I pinned him to the ground and grabbed his face with my hands. There was no resistance as I brought my mouth down on his. His energy had a different quality to it this time. It was no longer being forced into my body. I drew his energy into my core, feeling it buzz around my head and light up my body. There was an almost sour quality to his energy, not the sour milk kind, more the lemony taste that tightens your cheeks and makes you pucker. I wanted more of it.

My body relaxed into his as I drew more of his energy into me. It buzzed over me, causing my hair to stand on end. I could feel a lightness in my body and an odd sensation started developing in my core. It was something I had never felt before.

His energy wasn't being released like my other prey. It was like he was giving me a part of himself but holding on to the core of his being. I realized I wasn't sharing any of his memories or emotions. He was completely blank. I probed deeper but confronted a barrier as I reached for his core. Drawing back, I tried to build up my force and assaulted the barrier again. This time the resistance was almost painful. I gathered all my energy into myself, fighting his resistance. His mouth was locked onto mine and his hands were wrapped around my head. I brought my hands up and grabbed his wrists, trying to pry his grip from my hair. His wrist bones snapped and cracked in my grip, but he still held on to me. My head began to spin as his energy began to overtake me. I couldn't break his hold and I was losing control.

Suddenly I was free. I could feel hands lifting me off him and flinging me through the air. A sharp pain exploded in my head as I landed in a heap, huddled against the base of my rock. My stomach clenched and I pulled myself onto my hands and knees as I retched onto the ground. Stars exploded in front of my eyes and I blinked and shook my head to clear my vision. The priest was huddled on the ground while my family towered over him. I could see the brightness of their energy as they circled him.

I stepped forward to join my family, but father turned and shook his head at me. The priest stood up and rooted himself to the ground, taking a defensive position against my family. Father turned back to him, bringing the others into a tighter circle.

"Why are you here Hunter?" Father practically growled the words at him.

The priest smiled and looked directly at me. "Do you really need to ask me that?"

I could feel the others turn their attention to me although none of them turned to look in my direction.

"We protect our own, Hunter." Stephen said. "When you report back to your Warrior tell him he'll be facing a whole coven of us if he tries to attack our sister."

The priest held his hands up, his palms open and extended towards my father. "I have no intention of harming this child." His voice was soft and cajoling and I didn't believe him. "We are bonded, her and I. I could no longer harm her than I could cut off my right arm."

Cassandra lunged toward the priest her hands extended like claws. He reached forward and brushed her away as easily as if he was batting away a fly. She crumpled to the ground, screeching in pain.

Pulling myself to my feet, I stumbled towards her broken form. The others continued to circle around the Hunter. Stephen's energy was bleeding from his pores and oozing towards the man. I could see father attempting to step between them, but every time he moved towards Stephen the priest would make a gesture and father would stumble over his own feet. Cassie was still breathing, but barely. I crawled to where her body was sprawled out in the dirt. The others were putting up a valiant fight, but I knew they were going to lose.

Chapter Thirty

MY BODY ACHED ALL over. I felt every muscle and bone in my body and they were screaming at me where they had made contact with the rock. I don't know who had pulled me off the priest, but whichever one it was they did it with enough force to break a few things. I had suffered injuries before, but nothing like this.

Cassie's back arched as she tried to force air into her lungs. I brought my hand to her face and gently brushed her hair from her eyes. Blood was oozing from her ears and dripping from her nose. The whites of her eyes were completely red from burst blood vessels. I brushed my fingers across her lips, searching for her life force. My fingers came away smeared with blood. She reached up and grabbed my wrist, squeezing so hard my hand turned blue.

"Take me!" the words were barely discernable through the gurgle of blood in her throat.

Stephen was weakening, I could feel his life-force slowly leaching away from his body. Father tried to shore him up, but whatever power the priest was holding over my family was draining them too fast. My injuries were healing, but I wasn't going to be strong enough to join the battle before Stephen was completely drained.

Pain shot through my wrist as Cassie tightened her grip. She pulled me closer to her body. "Take me, now! Before it's too late."

Blood and spittle stained her lips, but I knew I didn't have time. I lowered my face and pressed my lips to hers. The metallic twinge to her blood caused the back of my throat to tingle. Her energy flowed into me, replenishing what I lost and giving me enough strength to heal my injuries. Hundreds of years of memories flooded into my brain, but they were jumbled and assaulted my senses with images beyond my comprehension.

Her memories cascaded into mine, colliding with images from my own past and twisted into a jumble of confusion I couldn't sort out. I tried to pull back, but she grabbed me and pulled me into her embrace. The taste of blood filled my mouth and I gagged on the feel of it. My entire body burned as the last of her energy flooded into me. Releasing me from her embrace, she fell back and crumbled into dust. The wind swirled around us, filling my eyes with the last bits of her existence. Gagging and retching, I spat the bitterness of her blood onto the ground and stood to confront the priest.

Stephen had collapsed to the ground. The front of his shirt was blood-soaked, but I could see the rise and fall of his chest. Helena was barely standing. Her entire body was swaying against the wind. Blood poured down her face, soaking her dress and turning her into a bright beacon of red.

I couldn't see how the priest could injure my family. He carried no weapon and he barely moved from where he stood rooted to the ground. Helena moved towards him, hands extended into claws. With a quick gesture, the priest threw a bright burst of energy from his hand, striking her in the chest. She collapsed to the ground without a sound. The priest turned and faced father.

The last of the pain was fading from my back and I could feel the strength flowing through me. Leaping from the ground I sprang at the priest's head. He didn't have time to react. I misjudged the distance and my strength and even though I knocked him down I ended up sprawled on the ground a few feet beyond him. Quickly scrambling to my feet, I spun around and crouched low to leap again. The priest made it to his feet before I could move. A sudden weight pressed down on me, rooting me to the spot. I could feel the strength of the priest as his energy pinned me to the ground.

Helena stirred. I could hear her groan as she rolled to her side. Sudden concern for her welled up inside me and I wanted to move to her side. Shifting my energy, I lashed out at the force pinning me to the ground. The priest staggered as the energy rebounded around him. The force holding me in place released its grip on me. Slowly, I peeled myself off the ground and adjusted my body into a crouch. My muscles were slow to respond and I felt clumsy, as if my body was fighting a war within itself. The priest turned his attention to me, leaving Stephen and Helena to writhe in the dust at his feet.

Father moved to Stephen's side and rolled him to his side. Stephen's body arched from the ground and a glottal scream reverberated from the core of his body. I reached out to him with my energy, but father blocked me from accessing his mind. Helena's energy was fading and I couldn't get to her. There was nothing more I could do for my family. I needed to turn my focus to the priest.

Bits of sand swirled around him creating a gritty cloak of glittering gold around his body. I could make out his smile through the cloud spinning around him.

"We will meet again, monster." The words were whispered, but I heard them clearly. "We belong to each other. Join us. We will hunt down the evil together."

A burst of wind sent sand into my eyes. I closed my eyes against the assault of grit. When I opened them he was gone.

My legs cramped and quivered as I moved towards my father and Helena. I only made it a few steps before collapsing to my knees. Crawling across the sand, I finally reached their huddled forms. Father had pulled his energy around him like a cloak. I grabbed the tail of his shirt but jerked my hand back when a shock buzzed my arm. I could feel father drawing away from me. His thoughts, usually so transparent, were dark and hidden.

I pulled myself against the monolith and huddled in the shelter it created. Father gathered Helena's limp form into his arms and turned toward the house. His eyes were dark and hooded as he looked my direction. I could feel anger and hatred vibrating off his energy. Flinching, I pressed my back into the rock and buried my face in my arms. I sensed father as he carried Helena into the house and returned for Stephen. Unburying my head, I watched as he lifted Stephen into his arms. As he turned to bring him back to the house I pushed myself up from the rock to follow.

Father shook his head as he repositioned Stephen. I could see the rise and fall of Stephen's chest, but the glow of his energy was so dimmed I wasn't sure if he was going to survive. He needed a large dose of energy and I was fairly buzzing with the abundance of life Cassandra had given me. Again, I attempted to stand, but father frowned and shook his head.

"Stay there, child." His voice was gentle, even though his face was darkened with repressed emotion. I saw anger, fear, pain, sorrow. More emotion than I ever experienced in my life. At least emotions I never felt on my own. I leaned my head back against the rock, allowing the heat from the baked stone to seep into my body and soothe the burning in my mind.

Cassandra buzzed around inside me, touching the deepest part of me. She flitted around my body like the butterfly she liked to emulate in her dance. I could feel her thoughts as she tried to bury herself in my memories. Thousands of years of experiences assaulted my senses.

My legs trembled as I forced myself up from the rock. I took a step forward, but my legs collapsed under me and I ended up crumpled in the dirt. This was worse than the old seizures. I was completely aware of the lack of control I was feeling in my muscles. I wanted the welcome darkness to embrace me, but it wasn't coming. Retching, I puked out the bitter taste of blood.

Curling up in a ball, I drank in the warmth of the sand under my cheek. The twinging in my muscles eased and the control slowly started to come back. I stretched out my limbs, flexing my fingers and toes until the tingling stopped and I could feel the warmth of the sand under my feet. I looked at my fingers. They looked strange, short and stubby and lacking all grace in movement. Forcing Cassandra back into the recesses of my mind, I refused to allow her to control my emotions. She was so mercurial in her energy. I breathed through the rush of emotions flooding through my body as I looked towards the house. The bright sun blinded me momentarily. Blinking, I forced away the tears gathering in the corner of my eyes. It was the first time in my life I could ever remember crying.

The tears dried quickly as I continued to force the emotions Cassandra had flooded me with into the back of my mind. She was still there, pushing the limits of my control. The others had kept her hunger in check, but now the drive to feed was inside me and was merging with my own hunger. I passed my tongue around the inside of my mouth, tasting the remnants of blood. The overwhelming revulsion I usually felt was tempered by Cassandra's cravings. I spit the taste into the sand, trying to eliminate the bitterness.

Pushing my back against the rock, I used its stability to push myself off the ground. I leaned into the rock balancing myself and allowing the world to stop spinning. I wanted to go into the house, but father was so insistent I stay in the garden I didn't move away from the rock. The world finally stopped moving long enough for my stomach to settle and my muscles to stop twitching. Cassie was finally pushed back into the area of my mind where I stored the lives of all my other prey. I needed to learn to filter her cravings and control them like I did the others bouncing around inside me.

Father was approaching from the house. I studied his expression, trying to read through the layers of fear and concern. He was carrying my backpack in his hand and he dropped it at my feet. A slow realization began to overwhelm me as I looked at the olive-drab pack at my feet.

"Father, no!" I reached out to embrace the man standing in front of me, but he stepped out of the way of my arms. A wrenching twisted in my chest as I felt the sharp pain of his rejection. Drawing into myself, I wrapped my arms around my chest and dropped to my knees.

Father crouched down on the ground in front of me but he still maintained a space between us. "Child, I can't touch you. I can't risk recreating the bond we have between us."

I reached for the bag and picked it up from the ground. There was barely any weight to it at all. Before I had a chance to open it father reached out and put his hand on the straps.

"You have everything you need in here," he said. "I'm really hoping we can bring you back soon, but there's enough in here to get you by for a long time."

Come back? Father wasn't making any sense. It was obvious he was sending me away, but he didn't intend for me to leave forever. I didn't understand what he was telling me.

Chapter Thirty-One

I FLIPPED THE TOP of my backpack open and dug through the contents. There were several my favorite hunting outfits rolled into tight bundles and wedged in together. Intermixed in the clothing was wads of money as big as my fist and held in rolls with rubber bands. The inside pockets held a dozen or so credit cards, all with my adopted name printed in bold letters.

Father kept a respectable distance from me, but I was starting to read the emotions in his face a little differently now. He was afraid. It wasn't an emotion I was familiar with, although many of my victims experienced it. Closing the bag, I slung it over my shoulder.

"Why do I need to leave?" I asked. "I didn't mean to take Cassandra. She gave herself to me. I'll give her to you if you want."

Father shook his head and took an involuntary step back. "No, we know she gave herself to you. It was the only way you could get enough strength to defeat the Hunter. We don't blame you and as long as you live Cassandra will always be a part of you. She will never die."

As he said the words I could feel Cassie pushing against the edges of my mind. She wasn't trying to escape. It was more like she was letting me know she was there. I almost smiled at the gentle nudge at the back of my mind, but the seriousness in father's eyes caused me to suppress the urge.

"How did he find me?" I thought I had escaped the Hunter. He obviously had ways to find me no matter where I hid.

Father sat down in the sand and studied my face for a few moments. "Sometimes I forget how very young you are. If you were raised among us you would know our histories. I think I have time to tell you. The Hunter is very young and you hurt him bad. He will take more time to heal from his wounds than we do. Contacting his Warrior is going to take him a lot of effort so we will be safe for a while."

I gathered my backpack close to my chest and sat down to listen to father. I had a feeling I hadn't heard the last of this Hunter. If I stood a chance of defeating him I needed to learn about my nemeses.

"The origins of the Hunters and the Warriors are lost in the histories, just as the beginning of humans and our own race are lost to legend," father explained. "Most legends say we all started from the same seed and diverged into the different species. Others have us born of the jointure of the daughters of God and the sons of Satan. It doesn't matter how we were born; all we know of each other is Hunter and prey. Our kind prey on the humans and their kind prey on us. It's all veiled in finely couched words of good versus evil, with our kind being the evil."

He almost reached out to me at that moment. I could see his hand twitch as if to touch my hair. Running my fingers through the short spikes, I imagined his fingers smoothing the unruly mess into some semblance of order, one of his favorite gestures. He curled his fingers into a fist before he touched me and brought his hand close to his chest.

"Hunters search out our kind and latch onto our energy." His voice was subdued and pregnant with regret as he continued his explanation. "They have the power to bind and injure us, weakening us for Warriors to come in for the kill."

Hunters, Warriors, Feeder, human. It was all a game of cat and mouse, but which one was the cat and which one was the mouse was all becoming a confusing mess.

"But, why do I have to leave?" I asked. "It took all of us to defeat this Hunter. If he finds me alone there is no way I will be able to take him on my own."

Father stood up in one graceful motion. "He won't harm you," he said. "He has latched on to you and your energy and has used you as an anchor. They're going after all your connections first. That's why I had to server our coven bonds. The creatures will separate us and take us out one by one if we don't protect ourselves. Right now, my coven has two options. We either band together and fight or sever our coven ties and hope they didn't get enough of a glimpse of our members to catch their scent."

I rested my chin on the top of my backpack and curled my legs towards my chest. Closing my eyes, I breathed in the scent of the desert. Cassandra's energy flashed through my mind and with it came the echo of her mother's bright thread of life. With a start, I opened my eyes and looked towards the house. I could sense Helena's waning energy as her life's force bled away.

"Helena's going to die, isn't she?" I asked.

"Probably," he replied. "It's touch and go with Stephen, too. And if the Warrior arrives before my other children, I will probably not survive the night. I can't force my children to come to our defense, but I can protect them from this fate. Those who come to my call will fight, and hopefully destroy this pair. The rest will have severed their connection with our coven and strike out on their own, at least until this threat has passed."

I pushed my backpack behind me and stood up to face my father. "I want to stay and fight, too."

His face reflected pride and sorrow as he studied me. "You can't, child." He said. "The Hunter has joined with you and can see what is in your mind. You need to separate yourself from us. If we destroy this Hunter and his Warrior our coven will be safe and you can return to us."

I choked back a sob. It surprised me because I had never felt this way before. Closing my eyes, I forced the tears back. Raging emotions flooded my mind, confusing my senses and sending my mind into turmoil. I could feel father close by, but his comforting energy was ebbing away from me. Taking a few deep breathes, I released the warmth of Cassandra's energy. Her strength flowed through me, calming my racing heart and allowing my mind to settle.

Opening my eyes, I studied father's stricken form. He was so quiet, his eyes hooded as he studied me. I stood up and slung my pack on to my shoulders.

"Where should I go?" I thought about heading back to Portland, but I knew it would be the first place the Hunter would look for me. A twinge in my mind reminded me he would always know where to find me. I could feel his energy swirling around inside my body.

"You can go wherever you want," he said. "I will always know where you are and will send for you when this danger has passed. Go where you can find plenty of prey. The Hunter and his Warrior won't seek you out until they've destroyed all of us and any other Were you have met. You're their connection to our world so they won't hunt you down right away. And with each battle they fight with us there's the chance we will be able to injure and kill them. You've hunted Were before. The Hunter and Warrior caste are just as fragile as we are. We can kill them, just as they can kill us."

"I wish I still had my motorcycle." I said. "It would get me far away from all of you quickly."

Father nodded, pointing at my back pack. "You have enough money in there to buy one, although you could always obtain one the same way you got your first one. I've never seen anyone as adept as hiding their energy from the humans as you are. You can hide in plain sight, if you wanted."

I thought about all the ways I had learned to hide from the humans. Shape-changing was one of my favorites, but an extension of my energy was the simplest method of hiding from them. I wanted to embrace father before I left, but I knew any physical contact with him would reestablish our connection. Turning my back on the house, I headed to the edge of the rock garden. The property line blurred into the hills above the city and I ran for a while before dropping back towards a populated area.

I climbed to the top of one of the hills and found a smooth, stout rock and sat down. The sun was just beginning to set over the tips of the mountain but the lights from the city brightened the sky, bathing the valley in an eerie glow. I allowed the beauty to flow over me as the breeze picked up, bringing the smell of the desert to my senses.

Tucking my backpack into a pile of rocks I made sure it was well-disguised and gathered my energy around my body. I hadn't changed form in a long time and I wanted to feel the world around me from a different perspective. Crouching low I picked up handfuls of sand and let it shift through my fingers. It was still warm from the heat of the day. Focusing the energy in my core, I pushed at the edges of my mind and pulled the form around me.

The city was behind me as I climbed farther into the hills. As the moon rose over the mountain I lifted my muzzle and sang to the shimmering light. Digging my claws into the earth, I ran as fast as I could. The sounds of humanity faded away and I was able to shed the weight of the battle from my mind. Wind stirred my fur, ruffling it into tufts and cooling my throbbing heart.

Cassie was laughing. I could feel her energy in my mind as I loped through the rock formations. Blood was rushing through my veins as my heart beat faster. I don't know how far I ran, but by the time I was done I could no longer see the lights of the city.

Despite the brightness of the moon, there was a quiet darkness settling about the land as I came to a rest at the edge of a cliff. Changing back to my natural form, I drew in deep, cleansing breaths waiting for my heart to settle back to normal. The light from the moon bathed over me and I flung my arms wide to draw in as much of the energy as possible.

I couldn't run away. My family needed me. I had never been close to anyone before and the idea of abandoning them to the mercies of Hunters caused my heart to contract. Turning my back on the moon, I changed back into the form of the wolf and made my way back to where I left my pack.

I had to change back to my own form to retrieve the pack. Lifting it over my shoulder, I headed back down into the city. I gave my old home a wide berth, trying very hard to not think about what might be happening within its walls. The chaos of the city grated on the edges of my energy and the brightness it usually held for me was missing. All around me all I could see was the muted colors of simple humanity. I missed the bright energy of my own kind. Even the members of Sebastian's coven seemed to be missing from the streets. If they were gathering for battle it wasn't going to happen in these streets. I needed to regroup. I needed a plan. There were plenty of places to hide in this city, I just needed to find a hole to crawl into for a while.

Chapter Thirty-two

I COULD BARELY FEEL my backpack against my shoulder blades as I raced throughout the city streets. There wasn't any weight to it without the cans of food I usually carried with me. I had stopped at a market a few hours ago, but I hadn't bothered getting any of the money out of the pack. I filled my pockets with apples and oranges and walked out the sliding glass doors. No one noticed me, they never do. Money was such a human concept. I could understand how most of my kind needed to bother themselves with this human convention. They needed shelter and food, a place to rest. I needed food too, but since I learned to hide myself from the eyes of the humans I knew I wouldn't have any problems obtaining what I needed. Most of my kind didn't have the ability to hide themselves from human eyes the way I did. The way father did. Maybe he could use his abilities to hide from the Hunter, if he was still alive. I tucked that thought away and focused on finding a place where I could hide.

Working my way through the maze of bodies on the street, I found myself outside of a darkened building. It was one of the many projects started during the building boom from a few years before and abandoned when the money ran out. In a few years someone would come along and finish it or knock it down and start another project. Right now, though, it offered me what I needed. I maneuvered my way around the barriers blockading the entrance to the underground garage and made my way through the dark maze to the elevator shafts at the back of the structure.

Only one of them was occupied. The man was deep in the throes of drug induced illusions and he wasn't even aware of what was happening when I drained his life-force from his body. His energy burned through my body, blurring with the others bound within my head. There wasn't much of his mind left and he tasted bitter. For a moment I wished I still had my seizures. It would have felt good to vomit the taste of him out of my body.

I dragged his body up about three levels and dropped it to the bottom of the shaft. By the time the mangled pile was found he would probably be unrecognizable. I crawled up the inside of the shaft until I reached the top floor of structure. The walls of the shaft were smooth and allowed very little purchase for my hands and feet. None of the internal workings of the elevator were in place and where the doors should have been were wide openings. I dropped from the top of the shaft into the sloped surface of the garage.

The sound of my footsteps echoed as I paced across the vast, empty space. I needed to clear my mind and figure out a plan, but there were too many people bouncing around in my head. The outer cement walls of the garage were broken up by great empty spaces. I could see the lights of the city glowing through the walls. Great cement columns supported the inner structure of the garage, giving a sense of permanence to the half-completed project. The walls and columns were painted with murals of spray paint, some more intricate than others. I knew enough about graffiti from the streets of Portland to know where to look for signatures.

Many of the tags were unfamiliar, but I recognized a few of the more common gang markers. It took a few moments to find one with recognizable coven markings. I didn't know whose coven the mark belonged to, but I knew it didn't belong in this territory. This garage was on the edge of my family's territory, an area Sebastian was trying to usurp. I ran my fingers over the markings. It was difficult to tell the age of the mark, it could have been there for years or months or even days. The artist could have made the mark and moved on or could have been killed in one of the many border battles being fought over this territory. A surge of anger boiled up inside me. This territory should never be in dispute. It belonged to my father and our coven. I knew the anger wasn't just mine. Cassandra was forcing her energy forward and her emotions were playing havoc with my own.

I pushed the thoughts of my family to the back of my mind. It wouldn't help them if I thought about their secrets with the priest bouncing around in my head. Gritting my teeth, I forced Cassandra back to recesses of my brain, tamping down the hot emotional surge she brought with her. I needed time. I needed to figure out what I was going to do. My body felt full and my skin tingled with the energy I had consumed. My belly was empty and I was reminded of the fruit in my pack. Sitting on the cold, cement floor I propped my back against a pillar and opened my bag.

The fruit filled my belly and the energy filled my body, but I still felt empty inside. I pulled my pack onto my lap and dug through the contents. I wasn't really looking for anything in particular, I just wanted to see what I was carrying away from the only place I ever really considered home. Clothes and money. It was all I had left of the time I spent with my adopted family.

There was an orange buried in the soft folds of a cotton shirt. Lifting the fruit to my nose, I inhaled the fragrance. A sudden craving tightened the back of my throat and I tore into the orange flesh, revealing the tender, juice-filled fruit beneath. I drained the juice just like I drained the energy from my last meal. The sweet juice filled my mouth and traveled down my throat, but it did nothing to satisfy the craving throbbing in my mind. Tossing the orange peel aside I arched my back and stretched to loosen my muscles.

The urge was still there. Cassie was pushing at the edges of my mind, letting me know she was hungry and only one thing would assuage her cravings. Flipping the top of my bag closed I stood up and repositioned it underneath me. I pressed my back against the pillar again and closed my eyes. Slowing down my breathing, I focused on controlling the energy coursing through my body. I needed to sort through the thoughts rolling through my head. My mind wouldn't settle and I couldn't think.

I had tasted other Were before, but none of them raged through my mind like Cassandra. Her appetites were stronger than anything I had ever experienced. She rivalled even my mother in her cravings. It was different with Cassie, though. With my mother I was outside of her mind. Cassie was inside me, trying to take over. I had to bend her to my own purposes. I couldn't allow her to control me.

She fought me. I was stronger than her, but she had thousands of years of experience on her side. She wanted my body as her own and she wasn't letting go. The more I tried to push her back the more she pounded at my mind. My limbs twitched with the force of her energy. I tried to stand but I couldn't pull myself to my feet and I ended up on my knees. Clenching my teeth, I forced her back.

"Cassie, stop it." I said the words out loud, even though I knew she couldn't hear me, but she could feel the power of my convictions.

"You can't beat him on your own." The words echoed in my head.

I kept pushing, trying to force her into the corners of my mind. My fingers and toes tingled with numbness as I forced myself to my feet. Cassie surged one more time, but I forced her back. I wasn't going to let her gain control of me.

Everything ached. I leaned against the pillar and drew in deep breaths. I forced her back and walled her into the deep recesses of my mind. She was still there. I would never be able to get rid of her, but I could control her, finally. A surge of warmth engulfed me, soothing my throbbing muscles and bringing strength to my body. I was filled with energy and strength beyond anything I ever experienced before.

Pushing away from the pillar, I stretched my muscles and pulled my body straight. The garage was a huge empty space and I couldn't resist the temptation. I had seen Cassie move often enough and I knew she was inside of me. My body wasn't as long as hers, but as I started to move around the broad expanse of space in the garage I moved with as much strength and grace as she did. The world was spinning under my feet and I controlled every inch of it. I didn't feel like I was moving in the world, I felt the world moving in me.

I had never really danced before, although I don't think it could have been called dancing since there wasn't any music. In fact, I don't think I ever moved without purpose before. There was freedom in this kind of movement and I began to understand what Cassie saw in it.

My most recent feeding left me with nothing more than a reserve of energy. There was no satisfactory burst of knowledge gleaned from his mind to trace its way into my subconscious. I could usually find some redeeming quality in my prey, but Cassie's presence was so overwhelming it was difficult to focus on anything else.

She was starting to quiet down and I turned my focus to the other brightly burning energy buried in my mind. He was still there, tracking me, searching for me. I looked for the edges of the presence, but I couldn't find it. Try as I might I couldn't isolate his energy from my own. He was there, inside my mind, forcing me to acknowledge him. I hated him. There was no doubt about that. I could feel the rage bubbling up inside me the more I thought about him.

The pillar became my only support as the energy tried to overwhelm me. He swam to the forefront of my consciousness. Grabbing the pillar with my hands I pushed into the unforgiving concrete. I could feel the penetrating stab of pain as his mind burrowed into mine. He was stuck to me like a burr digging itself into flesh. Every time I tried to force him away he dug in deeper. I used every reserve of energy I could, but the more I pushed the more he dug into my mind.

Blood mixed with dust ran down the pillar as my fingers shredded the cement. The pillar fought back, cutting my hands and snapping bones. I curled my hands into fists and swung. The pain shot up my arm but did nothing to dislodge the energy from my brain. He was there, consuming me, becoming a part of me.

Big shards of cement dropped from the pillar, groaning as they crashed to the floor. Stepping back, I studied the pile of bloody rubble at my feet. My hands throbbed as I uncurled my fingers. I needed to fix the broken ones so they would heal straight. The bones made a satisfactory snapping noise as I popped them back into place. As I watched the bruises faded, turning from black and purple to green and then healthy pink and white. I was perfect again. Perfect except for the man in my head, laughing at me.

Then he was there. His shadowy form stood between two pillars staring at me.

Chapter Thirty-Three

THERE WAS PLENTY OF room between the two of us. If I started running now there was no way he could catch me. I could run. I could survive. Stepping back from the column, I edged toward the broad opening leading to the street below.

"Wait!" his voice was commanding, but I didn't feel the pressure to obey that usually accompanied his demands. I stopped moving anyway.

"I'm not going to hurt you." He stepped into the light, stretching out his hand towards me. "Please, don't run away. I just want to talk to you."

I could feel him in my head, probing, searching. A low growl boiled up in my throat as I stared at him. He must have heard it because he stopped and returned my stare. The growl hadn't come from me. Cassie was pushing against the walls I had built around her.

"Listen," he said. "We don't have to be enemies."

The anger was back. It was so palatable I almost choked on it. He was standing there with his hand out to me, asking me to be his friend after he destroyed my family. I crouched low, digging my fingers into the pavement. He was smiling at me. There was no fear in his red-rimmed eyes.

"You will not attack me."

This time the command crashed down around me, nearly pinning me to the floor. I heaved my shoulders, forcing the compulsion off me. It was satisfying to see the smile slip a little. I was stronger than him. I returned his smile.

"I'm going to kill you this time." I forced the words out through clinched teeth.

The smile was back. "No, you're not," he said. "We are going to team up, you and I. We belong together."

"Never." The words were coming easier. "I belong to my coven. The coven you're trying to destroy."

"We're not going to destroy your coven." His tone was soothing, almost condescending. "Welhiem has rallied his forces. We can't reach him. There are other monsters we're going to hunt down and we want your help doing it."

"I'm not going to help you hunt down my own kind." I straightened up, squaring my shoulders against his assault.

"We are your own kind." He stepped close enough he could reach out and touch me if he tried. "In the beginning we all started out together. Your kind. My kind. His kind. We all started as one tribe, in the beginning. It's the only thing that makes sense." His hand reached towards my arm. I stepped back, revolted by the thought of his touch. "I don't understand a lot about this stuff. I didn't even know creatures like you, like us, existed. That creature, the one that killed your friends, he's teaching me about this world. It's all new to me. But, I understand some things. We need energy to survive. Not food. Humans consume food for energy. We consume souls."

"You?" I studied the man standing in front of me. His energy was clear of any shape-shifter energy. "You're not a feeder."

"We all feed on energy, we just all do it a little differently." His smile was even more condescending as he studied my face. "You saw it for yourself. The energy of the creatures the Warrior killed in your graveyard, you saw it go into his body. Oh, he doesn't acknowledge it. Do you know he doesn't believe me when I tell him he feeds on the souls of those creatures? Of course, I feed on them too. I've been following him around, taking his scraps and learning to feed."

"You and I are nothing alike." I didn't even bother disguising the hatred in my voice.

"We are," his voice was nearly a whisper. "You, me, him, your father, your grandfather, we're all the same."

His mention of my grandfather stabbed into me. It held me captive with more force than I had ever felt before. The only way he could have known about my grandfather was if he had plucked the information about him out of my brain.

"No," I spoke with such force he took a step back. "You don't get to talk about my family."

"I could be your family." His voice was soft, seductive, but it lacked some of the conviction it once held. "I can't blame you for the sins of your past. We don't blame the shark when it attacks the swimmer. It's just following its instincts. You're just following yours."

My whole body was shaking as I forced my anger into a dark, quiet place. I needed to get control. I could feel him slowly chipping away at my defenses.

"My sins?" I scoffed at him. "Don't you have to believe in something in order to be considered a sinner?"

"Overcome your instincts, child." He reached for me again. "You don't have to feed on these fragile humans. I'm just finding my way around this world but hunting down these evil creatures makes me stronger. It can make you stronger, too."

"I'm not evil and you're not a part of my world." I released Cassandra from the walls I had built around her. Fire flooded through my veins as I struck out at him. My fist connected with his chest and I felt the crunch of bones as my fingers shattered under his muscle. The force of blow thrust him across the length of the building. He came to a rest against a pillar on the far side of the structure. The hot scent of blood filled my nostrils and I could see large, liquid pools spreading out from under his back and streaming from his nostrils.

He was broken and bleeding, but I could still see the rise and fall of his chest. I knew if I left him alive he would hunt me down. The only way I would ever be free of him was if I killed him. A tiny twinge in my mind reminded me I may never be free from him again.

I snapped my fingers back into place as I approached his huddled form. His blood was a deep, rich red. So different from my own. My fingers trailed through his spilled blood as I grabbed for his shirt. A low moan escaped his lips as I brought my face closer to his. He smelled sweet. His energy. His blood. I wanted to drink it all in.

The sound of footfalls distracted me from his scent. I turned and stood over the top of him. He was mine. The scent of the others flooded the space. I could taste their energy on the tip of my tongue. Dozens of them melted from the shadows. I could see the over-glow of the coven pack in their energy. They weren't mine. None of them carried the thread I had come to recognize as belonging to my family.

For a moment the glow of the coven thread overwhelmed me, but it faded and I was able to discern the different energies of the figures encroaching upon me. They weren't very strong despite their numbers. None of them could match me in strength and power. Each of them on their own wouldn't be able to touch me, but together, just by their sheer numbers, I knew I was in trouble.

I crouched low over the form of the priest. They were coming for both of us. I could taste it in the air. My hand made its way to the cold metal hilt of the short sword strapped across my back. As I backed up against the post the creatures approaching us reaching for weapons from hidden folds in their clothing. The sword didn't give me enough of an advantage.

The priest coughed and stirred beneath me. I spared a glance at the man. His bright blue eyes were clouded with pain, but his gaze was steady and strong. A rip in his shirt revealed a dark blue bruise, but even as I watched the bruise was fading. His wounds were healing at the same rate as mine always did. It wouldn't take him long to recover enough to stand beside me. It still wouldn't be enough, the two of us against them.

My back was against the pillar so I knew they could only get to me on three sides. If the priest managed to recover enough from his injuries to stand beside me he could take one of my sides. I would only have one side and my front to defend. Of course, that depended on the abilities of the priest. And his willingness to fight with me.

They formed a semicircle around us. I scanned the crowd, silently numbering them in my head. Nearly thirty of the creatures were huddled together, staring at me with the lust of hunger in their eyes. I planted my feet and held the sword in front of me.

"What are you waiting for?" I shouted the question at them. "You're going to have to fight for your meal."

None of them moved. They all stood there, staring at me. With a sudden undulating movement, the semicircle split and Sebastian stepped through. His makeup was missing and he was wearing dark, close fitting clothes like my own. Somehow, he seemed smaller, as if the removing the makeup and costume shrunk him a little. His energy was still strong, nearly as strong as mine. He would be the one I needed to kill first.

The priest groaned as he slowly pulled himself from the ground. I couldn't spare him a glance. I could only hope he would be willing to stand beside me against the others.

Sebastian stepped closer as the circle closed around him. The energies of the others seemed to flicker and fade next to his brightness. He stretched his arms wide, gesturing to the gathered creatures around him.

"You should have joined me when I first offered." His voice still carried the strong flavor of smooth seduction as he approached me. "My coven will be stronger than Welhiem's ever was."

"Why would I want to become part of your coven?" I asked. "You're nothing more than cast-offs, the rejects not worthy of becoming part of father's coven."

I made sure my voice was loud enough to be heard in the far corners of the garage. I could hear the hissing of angry voices coming from the shadows. More of them were hiding in the darkness. Sebastian must have brought only his strongest to confront me. I sought out the light hidden in the shadows. There weren't many of them. Most of Sebastian's coven were focused on me and the priest now that he was on his feet.

"Father left you on your own." The derision in his voice was almost palatable. "His coven is falling apart. It's disintegrating around his ears right now. He should have stood by you and fought the Hunter and his Warrior. Instead he turned you out to the wolves."

The priest radiated warmth as he took a stance by my side. I reached out and placed my hand on his chest. A rush of energy burned down my arm and arched from my hand to his body. I could feel his gasp of breath as he took in my energy giving strength to his body.

"I am strong enough to take all of you." I growled out the words. "Take your followers and leave."

Sebastian threw back his head and laughed. "And who are you to tell me what to do? I am a God. These creatures follow me. I control their destiny and now I control yours." He brought his arms down in a wide, sweeping gesture. The circle tightened around him and the lights from the shadows joined them as well.

Chapter Thirty-Four

THE CIRCLE WAS COLLAPSING around me. Sebastian stepped back as his followers rushed towards me. I felt pressure from my side and the crowd collapsed to the floor with a sudden simultaneous groan. Those who didn't fall stumbled in their forward movement. I could see the shock and confusion in their faces as they looked at me. Sebastian was the only one of them looking past me to the man standing behind my shoulder.

"What are you?" He was afraid. I could hear it in his voice.

"Your destroyer."

The response was simple, but heavy with power and promise.

Sebastian gestured to his people. They were slow. I could see the sluggishness in their response. Their faces all reflected different levels of fear and pain. I turned to Sebastian and slowly smiled at him. I could see his confidence crack a little.

I drew my sword and brought it up to eye level and waved it back and forth. The metal gleamed in the bright lights filtering in through the wide openings in the walls. Pointing the sword at the closest creature, I gave him a wide grin. His eyes narrowed and he took a step towards me. Sebastian held up his hand and the man stopped his forward motion.

"I haven't gotten your answer, yet." He reached towards me, his hands extended palms out and his fingers splayed wide. Waves of warmth and energy flowed from him and bathed over me. The smile he gave me was supposed to be soothing. It was meant to lull me into submission and give him an aura of trustworthiness, but I could see the twisting deception beneath his façade. I was not fooled.

I brought the sword point up so it was aimed directly at his chest and returned his smile. "It's not going to work." I whispered. "I see you. I know you. I will never become one of your lackeys." The words didn't need to be loud, he was the only one who needed to hear me.

His lip curled in a snarl and a growl rumbled from deep in his throat. "I will drain the last of your energy from your bleeding body myself."

With a gesture he released his sycophants on me. Another burst of energy buzzed by me from behind, causing the wave to collapse upon itself. A couple of Sebastian's followers managed to break the binding of the priest's energy and come within reach of my sword. A few quick slashes brought them, bleeding, to my feet. I grabbed one by the front of his shirt before he could collapse to the ground and brought my lips to his. As his life's blood spilled from the gaping wound in his chest I drained the energy from his body. His body crumbled to dust and I dropped his shirt on to the ground in front of me. The others writhed in pools of their own blood, groaning from the pain of their wounds. More of Sebastian's followers rose from the ground. I could see the sideways glances they gave their leader as they slowly crept back towards the shadows.

Sebastian hissed and gestured again. A few of his followers rallied and moved towards us, but I could sense the hesitation in their energy. The shine of silver from my blade was replaced by the slick red of the blood of my opponents. I could feel the warmth of the liquid dripping down the hilt and coating my hand. The muscles on my jaw tensed at the anticipation of the flavor, but I resisted the temptation to bring the blade to my mouth and lick it clean. It wasn't my craving. It was Cassandra's.

The priest knelt beside one of my other victims, placing his fingers over the woman's eyes. For a moment I thought he was going to close her eyelids, but instead I saw the bright flash of energy travel from her face, into his hand and up his arm. It was over in moments and as he stood the woman's body crumbled to dust.

There was still another one writhing at the base of the column. With one, swift motion I brought my blade down across his neck and kicked his head towards the crowd. The resulting explosion of dust scattered and settled on faces and arms of Sebastian's followers. Bright energy scattered up my spine and exploded in my head. Sebastian's growl deepened, but his followers seemed to shrink back even farther.

"Looks like you might have a few apostates." I waved my sword again and then brought it up to point directly at Sebastian. "Let's end this here. Come on, Sebastian. It's time to show your followers the face of God."

His quick gesture sent a few more of his followers forward. This time the priest allowed a few more of them to breach his defenses and make their way into range of my sword. I didn't bother trying to leave them alive. As I sliced with my sword clouds of dust exploded around us. One of the attackers went down in a heap at my feet. I watched his energy slowly fade from his crumpled body. It coalesced in the air just above his form. Turning into a ball of snapping energy, it floated about three feet into the air and flew across the room to a form hidden deep in the shadows.

Only a few of Sebastian's coven members watched the path of the energy ball. The rest of them were focused on me and my blade. I doubted many of them could even see the lights of the auras glowing so brightly around their forms. I stepped forward, nearly tripping over the body of the man I had just killed. He must have not had very much Were blood in him because he didn't dissolve into dust like the others.

The Warrior stepped out of the shadows and a few more of Sebastian's followers turned towards him. Sebastian kept his focus on me either unaware or unconcerned about the creature approaching at his back. A wave of panic was cresting over the crowd massing around Sebastian and the tension in the air became almost palpable. I licked my lips and savored the slightly acrid taste of dust, blood and fear. The edges of Sebastian's coven melted away as some of his people tried to retreat into the shadows. Sebastian's eyes darted to the side and finally turned to look at the Warrior. He barely glanced at him before turning his focus back on me.

"Are you switching loyalties?" Sebastian asked. "Or are the Hunter and the Warrior here for you?"

The Warrior smiled and unwound a length of metallic rope from where it was wound around his torso. "I will destroy all of you." His rich voice echoed off the walls of garage and reverberated through the space.

The priest was at my side. Sebastian and his followers were between me and the Warrior. And the Warrior was staring at me as if he wished he could drill holes through me with his eyes alone. I think I probably had about a zero percent chance of getting out of this one alive.

There was still the pillar at my back. Shoving the priest aside, I dug my fingers of my free hands into the cement and climbed to the ceiling. Sebastian lunged forward and tried to follow me, but a wall of energy forced him back. Despite the strength of my push, the priest was still on his feet and stood between the pillar and Sebastian's coven. A handful of them tried to separate from the crowd and dart towards the shadows, but the Warrior's metal whip caught them before they made it. He was fast. Maybe even faster than me. The few who might have made it collapsed against another impenetrable wall. Their bodies exploded into dust as soon as the sharp edges of the whip caught them and severed heads from bodies.

I sheathed my sword so I could get a better grip on the pillar. The microscopic crevices in the ceiling allowed my fingers and feet the purchase I needed to observe the scene below me. Sebastian barked a short, harsh order and his coven scattered. At first, I thought they were all running away, and perhaps a few of them were, but I could see they were making a wide circle around their leader. The priest and the Warrior stood outside the circle, each crouched low as the circle tightened around Sebastian.

I inched my way across the ceiling until I was directly above him. His eyes followed me and I smiled as slow realization dawned on his face. I pushed my tongue between my teeth as I smiled at him, savoring the taste of his fear. It all happened at the same instant. I dropped from the ceiling just as the priest and the Warrior leapt into motion. Landing on the balls of my feet, I drew my sword and sliced at Sebastian.

He got in a few good slashes, but he was no match for me. I could feel Cassandra throbbing in my head as I cut ribbons out of his chest and face. Like a cat teasing a mouse, I let him get out of the reach of my sword, briefly, then drew him back within my grasp. He gasped as I sliced deeply into his thigh and again when I thrust deep into his stomach. The dagger he had been using to defend himself fell to the ground with a clang and he huddled to the ground, covering his head with his arms. I kicked him hard in the side and sent him sprawling.

The others were all dead or dying. Dust coated my shoes turning them a silty-grey color. Bodies sprawled across the floor, lying at awkward angles, blood pouring from gash marks on their bodies. Sebastian lay at my feet, his broken body shuddering while his pale lips peeled back from bright, white teeth.

"You are with them?" His voice was weak, but I could hear the scorn it carried. "They destroyed your coven. They'll destroy you."

I grasped the sides of his face and pressed my lips against his. He was still too powerful and his energy refused to release itself from his body. His knife was only inches from my hand. I picked it up and buried it in his ribcage, piercing his heart. Blood gurgled in his throat as I drew his energy out of his body. Sweet, hot fluid filled my mouth and I swallowed all of it.

His body disintegrated into dust, collapsing in on itself and mingling with the blood and dust of the others. When I stood up from where I had bent over Sebastian the only other living creatures in the garage were the priest and the Warrior. A crosswind stirred the dust, causing it to blow into my face. I brushed my hand across my eyes and cleared the dust from my throat.

The priest was bent over one of the bodies that hadn't disintegrated into dust. For a moment I thought the woman wasn't quite dead, but her aura was completely dark. The priest dragged her body close to the pillar and piled it with the other two who hadn't turned to dust. The Warrior bent over the pile of bodies and placed his hands against them. Dark grey smoke spilled out from under his hands and spread over the bodies. Where the smoke touched the bodies, they withered and collapsed. Within moments the bodies were gone and the blackened particles of ash blended with the grey ash of the others. The wind blowing through the openings in the walls wiped away all the evidence of the battle we had just fought.

The Warrior turned on me. I could see the glow of his eyes as they burned into my core. The hunger was there. The hate. The anger. He wanted me dead.

Chapter Thirty-Five

I WAS AT THE elevator shaft in just a few steps. I didn't even bother with the footholds on the wall. I cast myself off the ledge and allowed myself to free fall to the bottom. Cassie's strength and natural balance allowed me to land with ease at the bottom of the shaft. My foot landed on the arm of the twisted body I had discarded earlier. His flesh had hardened and his face was twisted into a mask of pain. I got the impression it was an expression he had made often.

There was no time to pause and spend with a discarded shell. Gathering as much energy as I could, I pushed away from the body and raced across the concrete towards the street. They were there before I made it to the exit.

A sudden wave of pressure assaulted me, forcing me to stop. I pushed against the priest's restraints, but he held me bound to his will. I could see the glint of light on the Warrior's whip as he swung it around his head. Like a lamb to the slaughter. I gathered all my energy and pushed against the priest's binding. Bands of energy tightened around me, choking me and forcing me to my knees. I refused to bow my head and submit to death. Pain shot through my neck and radiated around my head, but I kept my eyes forward, staring directly into the dark face of the Warrior. His arm dropped and the whip fell in coils at his feet, but he still held my death in his eyes.

"Let me go, Hunter." He never took his eyes off me as he spoke to the priest. "You dare to use your powers against me?"

The priest moved to stand between me and the Warrior, holding up his hands as if to make a bridge between the two of us.

"She doesn't have to die," he said. "She's not like the others. Don't you see, if we teach her, if we show her how to fight, she can become a great Warrior?"

The Warrior's eyes narrowed as he continued to stare at me. I could see the muscles in his neck and chest strain as he tried to fight the binding holding him. The bands holding me in place were starting to slacken. I realized as I relaxed my muscles the bands loosened. If I could lull the priest into a sense of security I could attack both him and the Warrior while they were distracted. I relaxed the muscles in my neck, allowing my chin to drop to my chest.

The Warrior growled and I heard him struggle against the priest's binding. I could feel the binds holding me loosen even more. It wouldn't be long now. A bolt of warm energy flowed through me and I gasped as the priest laid his hand on my head. Strength filled me and the bindings slipped away.

Rising from the floor, I slipped the last of the bonds away and faced the Warrior. He stood before me, bound and helpless. The priest stood between us his arms spread wide and energy snapping from his fingers. I drew my sword and held it towards the Warrior.

"Put it down." He nearly whispered the words but I couldn't ignore the compulsion in his voice. I lowered the sword. "Do you feel the strength pouring through your body? The souls of humans can never give you this kind of strength. Come with us. I'll show you how to really use your power."

I gestured towards the Warrior. "And every time I turn my back he'll be trying to kill me."

"No, he won't."

"Yes, I will." The Warrior spoke through clinched teeth. "Release me, Hunter. Let me do what I need to do."

"No, you won't." The priest turned to the Warrior. "The two of us alone can't take on the strongest of these creatures. We wouldn't have been able to kill that coven leader if it wasn't for her. We still can't get to the old one and his coven. She can help us."

"I won't help you kill my family." I tried to bring the sword up, but it was too heavy in my hand.

"We're not going after your coven, at least not yet." The priest raised his hand and the blue light sparked off his fingers. "We have others to go after. Can't you feel the power flowing through you? If you join us I can give you that power."

Energy was flowing through my body. I felt as if everything from the top of my head to the bottom of my feet was on fire. Even my hair follicles vibrated with energy. I burned. I felt alive.

"What about him?" I nodded towards the Warrior.

"He won't kill you." The priest said. "I promise."

The bands of energy holding the Warrior dropped away. I still couldn't raise my sword in my own defense.

"Let me go, priest." I said. "I'm not going to stand here and let him kill me."

The priest shook his head. "We're going to become a team. It's time we started to trust each other."

The energy arching across his hands faded and he lowered his arms. He walked to one of the pillars and picked up a bundle tucked against the base. "I brought this down with me. You're going to need it." He dropped my backpack at my feet. "We'll be waiting for you."

He turned and walked towards the exit of the garage. The Warrior glared at me. I tightened the grip on my sword. He dropped his gaze and turned and followed the priest.

I reached down and picked up my backpack. It was light and smelled slightly of oranges. I cleaned off the sword and sheathed it. Sliding my pack on to my back, I adjusted it over the sword. The Warrior stepped out on to the street and turned the corner. I could still feel the Hunter's energy buzzing around my head. They would be gone in just a few minutes and I would be on my own again. Cassandra pushed against her walls and the cravings rolled up from inside. Forcing her down, I turned towards the exit. The lights from the street were so bright I couldn't tell if it was day or night. I could hear the priest's voice calling to me from inside my head.

The energy overwhelmed me, filling me with strength. Cassie and Sebastian and the other Were I had fed upon buzzed within my veins. I was strong. It was beautiful. I allowed Cassie's energy to flow through me. Sebastian cried out to be released. Laughing, Cassie twisted around him and engulfed his strength. I let her play for a minute, then I pushed her back into her place.

The siren's song called to me. There were so many of them out there. So much energy I could make my own. If the priest could lead me to them. If I could protect my family by joining them. I could follow him to the ends of the earth. I was strong enough for this. And when the time came I would be strong enough to kill them both. Shrugging my backpack into place, I followed the Warrior and the Hunter into the street.

I hope you enjoyed this book. Please take a few minutes to post an honest review. Thank you.

About the Author

Lucinda Moebius has been a writer since she was a child and was first published in 2010. Since then she has worked hard to create unique visions and stories. Her work includes novels in multiple genres including: Science Fiction, Fantasy, Paranormal, Children's Books, Screenplays and Non-fiction. Lucinda has a Doctorate in Education and loves teaching, but her greatest desire is to help others understand how literature and writing can bring enlightenment and understanding to everyone. She offers book coaching and advice to everyone, whether they want it or not.

Other Books by this Author

Echoes of Savanna: Book One: The Parent Generation

Raven's Song: Book One: T1 Generation

Write Well Publish Right

Publish Promote Repeat

Feeder: Chronicles of the Soul Eaters Book 1

Hunter: Chronicles of the Soul Eaters Book 2

30 Days Stream of Consciousness

Haunting

Abduction

Fire and Ice a Love Story

-- in Between